"Stop acting like this is another investigation."

Mercedes grabbed Jeremy by the shoulders. "It's not. It's your life. Someone wants to kill you."

"If that were true I'd be dead by now."

"How can you be so detached about this?" The warmth of her hand set his cheek aflame. "We're partners. You have to trust me."

"I can't." He'd trusted deeply once, and had been betrayed. "I haven't had a lot of luck trusting people."

She turned and stared him down. "I'm not just people. I'm your partner."

A partner he wanted to kiss at the moment...

PAT WHITE

the ENGLISH DETECTIVE *and the* ROOKIE AGENT

TORONTO • NEW YORK • LONDON
AMSTERDAM • PARIS • SYDNEY • HAMBURG
STOCKHOLM • ATHENS • TOKYO • MILAN • MADRID
PRAGUE • WARSAW • BUDAPEST • AUCKLAND

Thanks to Karen Galvin, reader, adviser and friend.

ISBN-13: 978-0-373-69241-5
ISBN-10: 0-373-69241-2

THE ENGLISH DETECTIVE AND THE ROOKIE AGENT

This edition published by arrangement with Harlequin Books S.A.

www.eHarlequin.com

Printed in U.S.A.

ABOUT THE AUTHOR

Pat White has been spinning stories in her head ever since she was a little girl growing up in the Midwest, stories filled with mystery, romance and adventure. Years later, while trying to solve the mysteries of raising a family in a house full of men, she started writing romance fiction. After six Golden Heart Award nominations and a *Romantic Times BOOKreviews* Award for Best Contemporary Romance (2004), her passion for storytelling and love of a good romance continue to find a voice in her romantic-suspense tales. Pat now lives in the Pacific Northwest and she's still trying to solve the mysteries of living in a house full of men—with the added complication of two silly dogs and three spoiled cats. She loves to hear from readers, so please visit her at www.patwhitebooks.com.

Books by Pat White

HARLEQUIN INTRIGUE

944—SILENT MEMORIES
968—THE AMERICAN TEMP AND THE BRITISH INSPECTOR*
974—THE ENGLISH DETECTIVE AND THE ROOKIE AGENT*

*The Blackwell Group

CAST OF CHARACTERS

Jeremy Barnes—A reserved detective assigned to find a missing boy while training a new agent for the Blackwell Group, Jeremy is not one to show his emotions, for fear they'll be used against him.

Mercedes Ramos—A former FBI agent who fears her passionate nature will always get in her way and hold her back from being an analytical detective.

Lucas Weddle—Lost ten-year-old boy, Lucas is the son of a self-made millionaire. Was the boy kidnapped or the victim of an accidental drowning?

THE BLACKWELL GROUP:

Max Templeton—Director of the Blackwell Group, Max pairs Jeremy with Mercedes to create balance in his lead investigative team.

Cassie—Max's assistant and girlfriend.

Eddie Malone—Computer geek extraordinaire.

Joe Spinelli—Chicago cop turned private investigator.

Bobby Finn—Formerly of Scotland Yard.

Chapter One

A woman was standing over him.

It couldn't be. He was hallucinating.

Jeremy Barnes rolled over on the hotel bed and groaned. This was worse than any hangover he'd experienced during his early days at university. He moved slightly and his muscles ached in protest.

What the hell had happened? He opened his eyes, but couldn't read the clock without his glasses. He hated feeling this weak, out of control.

Must be some sort of flu, he thought, closing his eyes and focusing on taking deep, slow breaths. He'd felt fine last night. He ground his teeth. He should be out there looking for the boy who'd gone missing off the Oregon coast.

Instead, he lay in a sweat-drenched bed.

"Bollocks." He swung his feet to the floor and gripped his head. It pounded a blaring verse of "God Save the Queen."

"You finally ready to get up?"

His eyes snapped open at the sound of the woman's voice. Blast, he hadn't been hallucinating. A tall female stood not five feet away from him.

"What the hell are you doing in my room?" he said.

His firearm—where was it? He reached for his weapon on the nightstand, but instead knocked over the water bottle. His fingers trembled. Like he'd be able to shoot, much less aim the bloody thing.

"Rough night?" she said, a slight accent to her voice.

He found his glasses on the nightstand and placed them on the bridge of his nose. The female came into focus—tall, slim with tan skin and round dark eyes—eyes that burned fire.

"You with the hotel staff?" he asked. Who else would have access to his room?

She narrowed her eyes. "And if I were blond with blue eyes you'd ask me that same question?"

"Excuse me?"

"No, I'm not hotel staff," she said. "Your boss sent me."

"Max sent you?" He stood, but the floor shifted and he sat back on the bed. "I'm late?" He ran his hand through his hair.

"I'd say so. It's almost noon."

He glanced at the clock. He'd been asleep for more than twelve hours. He usually never slept more than six.

"We expected you hours ago," she said. "You didn't answer your phone. Must be some hangover."

Hangover? The woman assumed too much. Jeremy was not one to overindulge. He was in control. At all times.

She seemed fascinated by his personal items, flipping open his wallet with her pen, then poking at his university ring.

He wanted to order her to get away from his things and get out, but he was still struggling to get his bearings and figure out what the hell was the matter with him.

He'd only had half a glass of wine with dinner, a mild red to complement his beef tenderloin. The Blackwell Group seemed healthy enough last night. Leader, Max Templeton, was his usual demanding self; Eddie Malone was lighthearted, but focused; and Bobby Finn and Joe Spinelli were anxious to get started on finding the boy.

What was his name again? Jeremy pinched the bridge of his nose. Bugger. What was his name?

"Are you coming or what?" she said.

He glanced at her. "Who are you?"

"Mercedes Ramos. Your new partner."

It couldn't be.

She reached out and shook his hand, vigorously. His head ached.

He retrieved his hand and studied her.

"You looked so shocked," she said. "What, you

think a Puerto Rican girl is only good for cleaning your room?"

"I didn't realize—"

"What that I'm Latina? That bothers you?"

"No, it doesn't." What bothered him was he didn't know his partner was a woman, a gender he had trouble communicating with on a good day.

"I'm sorry about the misunderstanding." He wanted to ease that tense look on her face, that look that meant he was in for more verbal sparring. He didn't have the energy for it.

"More likely you're sorry you drank too much whiskey last night."

He stood. "I did not overindulge."

The room went into a full spin. He grabbed the headboard for support. "Tell Templeton I'm on my way."

She sighed. "I was ordered not to come back without you." She knelt beside his minifridge. "Got anything good in here?"

"I wouldn't know," he said, rubbing his temples.

"Oh, I think you would." She swung open the door to reveal it was half empty.

He hadn't paid any attention last night when he'd checked in. The hotel staff must have forgotten to restock it before he'd arrived.

"Even the booze is gone," she said, holding up an empty liquor bottle. "You had a party and didn't invite me? I'm hurt." She stuck out her lower lip in a pout.

She was playing with him. Jeremy Barnes did not play—at anything. "Get the hell out of here."

"Now you swear at a woman? I thought Englishmen had better manners."

"You break into my hotel room and accuse me of having bad manners?"

"I didn't break in." She leaned against the dresser, arms crossed over her chest. "The maid let me in."

Grinding his jaw, he swiped a shirt and trousers from his open suitcase on the dresser and made for the bathroom. He slammed the door and locked it. Max said he'd found a new promising agent, but why pair this pushy female with Jeremy?

Max knew Jeremy worked best alone.

They didn't need a new team member to complicate things, especially when a boy's life was at stake. Why the change in team structure? Blast, Jeremy had created Blackwell, found the right combination of professional investigators to solve crimes quickly and efficiently. Why had Max made this crucial decision without Jeremy?

Because Max was worried about him. He'd said as much last week when the doctor discharged Jeremy from the hospital. Max had looked at him strangely and asked if he needed a holiday, maybe a few weeks rest on a beach.

Sounded tempting, but not now, not when a boy was missing. Maybe this one he *could* save.

Jeremy ran the cold water in the sink and stared at his reflection in the mirror. He looked one step away from death with pale white skin and bloodshot eyes.

It didn't matter if he was dying. A boy was out there, scared and alone.

Jeremy would not abandon him.

"*DIOS MIO*," MERCEDES WHISPERED. Multiple bottles of alcohol, candy and snack wrappers, along with a crumpled pack of cigarettes filled the garbage can.

God was punishing her by partnering her with this man. She paced the room and stared out the second story window at the ocean. Calm, peaceful waves danced onto the Oregon shore, so opposite from the storm brewing in her chest.

She'd busted her tail to get on the Blackwell team, finally breaking through Templeton's objections by agreeing to do him a favor—keep an eye on Jeremy Barnes.

Templeton didn't say why, but she sensed the importance of this assignment. She wondered if he thought Agent Barnes had gone bad.

She had done her research before joining the team. During his years with Scotland Yard, Barnes had had an impeccable reputation as an analytical thinker, a brilliant man with sharpened investigative skill. She thought she could learn from him, perfect her own skills, maybe even join this team of elite investigators and bypass all the chauvinistic garbage of a government agency.

She wanted to be equal with the men in her field, to prove to her little sister, Ivy, that a woman's worth was not dependent on how beautiful she was, or how well she cooked.

Old voices taunted her. *Make my dinner, Mercedes. Iron Papi's shirts, Mercedes. Clean up Juan's mess, Mercedes.* Ordered all the time. Expected to wait on the men like they were special.

When she'd announced her plans for college—not marriage—Papi had told her not to reach beyond her abilities. She'd only be disappointed.

Maybe she should have chosen another line of work, one that wasn't so heavily populated by men. But her gender shouldn't matter. She was smart and hardworking. That should be what counted most.

It wasn't. Being an attractive female had nearly gotten her fired from the FBI. Because she was female, her partner, Will Crane, felt it necessary to put his life in danger to protect her, making her look inept. Because she was female, everyone jumped to conclusions when the first word out of his mouth after he awakened from the surgery was, *Mercedes.*

Of course, wifey assumed her husband and Mercedes had been having an affair, so she let the boss have an earful—in front of the rest of the division. They all knew Mrs. Crane didn't appreciate her husband being partnered with an incompetent agent who couldn't take care of herself, an agent who had seduced her husband.

Mercedes tried to ignore the looks from the rest of the guys in the office that day, and the day after and the day after that. Although wifey's accusations weren't true, it was too easy to believe, and Mercedes had been marked for a desk job.

She'd been burned. Again. She hadn't even had the pleasure of romance and love.

More like pleasure and pain.

Michael. She sighed.

He'd been the first man she thought had treated her with respect, yet he'd just wanted to sleep with her. She'd been sheltered and naïve thanks to her strict upbringing. After the Michael disaster, she'd learned never to mix work with romance. Which was why the accusation of having an affair with Crane was ridiculous. But it didn't matter. She still got burned.

¡Basta! Stop thinking about the past and get your head in the game—playing nursemaid to a pathetic drunk.

"Four months of hell, chica."

She'd follow Barnes around, pick up after him and record his mistakes, all the while working to find a lost boy.

Why hadn't Templeton fired the man?

Because of the good old boys' network, right?

Damn, she half hoped to find Barnes doing something illegal so Templeton would shove him behind a desk. That would allow her to focus on her real job—finding Lucas Weddle.

Instead, she found Jeremy Barnes half-naked and barely able to stand.

She had to admit he was wildly attractive. His broad chest and stomach looked hard from weights and sit-ups. She hadn't dared let her gaze wander any lower.

Heat rose to her cheeks. Pretty pathetic that she was lusting after a man like Barnes. *Talk about intentionally torching your career.*

But she was a healthy woman in her prime. She hadn't been close to a man for more than five years and intended to keep it that way, especially with men at work.

What was taking Barnes so long? She knocked on the bathroom door. "Did you fall in?"

Nothing.

"Barnes!"

The bathroom door swung open. "Do you have to yell like a high school cheerleader?"

He pushed past her looking nothing like the man who'd practically fallen on the floor a minute ago.

"I need tea," he said, pouring water into the coffeemaker.

"Tea?" she said. *What kind of wimp drinks tea?*

"I suppose you drink coffee, no cream or sugar?" he said.

"And if I do?" She made it stronger than anyone else at her FBI field office.

"You'll have an ulcer by the time you're forty," he said.

"Who are you to talk? You drink booze like water and lecture me about drinking coffee?"

He took a step toward her. Although he was still a foot away it felt like he was right on top of her.

His blue eyes narrowed. "I told you, I do not over-indulge in alcohol."

"Then who consumed most of your minibar, the booze fairy?"

"They must not have restocked it from the previous guest."

"Uh-huh."

"Does everything have to be a battle with you?" he asked, stretching out his neck.

She resented the inference. It reminded her of childhood tormentors taunting, *Mad Mercedes, bad Mercedes. Always picking fights.*

"I'm just stating the facts," she said.

"Well, Agent Ramos, you've got your facts wrong. I hope that's no indication of your future performance for Blackwell."

Intimidation? From this guy?

"Blackwell, right, the agency that's supposed to be finding Lucas Weddle." *Instead of sleeping until noon.* She let the inference fall between them.

He blinked and she could have sworn a glint of sadness colored his eyes.

Turning away from her, he pulled a baggie out of his suitcase and flicked it with his finger. Hell, if that didn't look like…

"Roll your own, do you?" she said.

"One doesn't roll tea. One steeps it."

He *had* to be kidding. Great, her partner was an alcoholic tea snob.

He placed a metal strainer over a foam cup, shook some tea leaves into it, then poured in the hot water.

All that for a stinkin' cup of tea?

"You should try it," he said, reading her mind.

More like her expression. Papi always said he could read her like a *Tribune* headline.

"I'll pass," she said.

He turned to her. "Bring me up to speed."

Just like that she was supposed to forget she'd found him barely functioning with a hangover. Just like that she was expected to give him control of their portion of the case. He treated her like his secretary. She was getting tired of this routine.

Pulling out her notebook she started, "Lucas Weddle, ten, from Mountain View, Oregon. Missing three days. Last seen at the beach where he was on a school field trip."

"Didn't they do a head count before boarding the bus?"

She flipped through her notes. "Yes, the teacher's assistant counted twenty-three students."

"The teacher's assistant, what do we know about her?"

"Nancy Boyd, thirty-eight, married thirteen years, two children. Nothing unusual or extraordinary about her."

Nothing extraordinary, kind of like Mami, but not like Mercedes. She'd make something of her life and prove she was as capable as any man, that she deserved to be treated with respect.

"What have the authorities done so far?" He pulled the strainer out of the cup.

She couldn't help but notice his long, slim fingers tremble as he placed it on the coffee tray.

"The local task force did a thorough search of the area and have enlisted the help of the Coast Guard dive team. They expanded the search boundaries a mile north and south of where the boy was last seen."

"No one noticed the boy had gone missing?" He placed a lid to his cup and turned to her.

"No. He was a shy kid, mostly kept to himself."

"Hmm." He sipped his tea, an odd look on his face.

He was a hard one to read and Mercedes didn't like surprises.

"Well, let's be off, then." He opened the hotel room door and cringed at the brightness of daylight.

"Sure you don't want some aspirin with your tea?" She ambled past him welcoming the sun's warmth.

"You're going to keep at me all day, aren't you?" He followed her to the car.

She hesitated. "I'll drive so you can concentrate on holding your cup steady."

She'd crossed the line. She knew it. Damn her uncontrollable mouth.

He narrowed his eyes. "It's a good thing you pursued a career in law instead of medicine."

"Why?"

"You've got as much compassion as a serial killer." He opened the passenger door and slid into the sedan.

She wished she had a sassy remark at the tip of her tongue. But what could she say? That she'd used up all her compassion on a draining family and constant battles in a sexist career? No, this man didn't need to know her struggles.

Swiping her hand through long, dark hair, she took a deep breath. Having driven all night to get here wasn't such a good idea. She was irritable about having to be a babysitter instead of an investigator.

For some strange reason Barnes got to her. No one had gotten to Mercedes Ramos in many years.

She got behing the wheel and glanced at her partner. He rested his head against the seat, his hand clutching his cup, his breathing steady. Had he passed out?

"What about the parents?" he asked, not opening his eyes. "Did they notice anything unusual in the boy's behavior lately?"

"Nothing." She pulled out of the lot and headed for the Command Center, an office in a storefront on Main Street.

"Brothers and sisters?"

"A younger sister."

"Friends?" he asked.

"Not really."

"A shame," he whispered.

They drove a few blocks in silence.

"And what about you?" he queried.

"I have friends."

He opened his eyes and narrowed them at her. "Really?"

Was he teasing her?

"What I meant was, what brought you to Blackwell?" he clarified.

"Didn't you read my file?"

"There wasn't a file. Just Templeton's directive that I train you."

She stiffened. *He* was going to train *her?*

"You were with the FBI?" he said.

"Five years."

"You plan to return?"

"Possibly." He didn't have to know that her reputation had been ruined thanks to a protective partner and jealous spouse.

"Why the break?"

"I'm off to recover." Ah, bad choice of words.

"Recover from?"

"None of your business."

"I beg to differ. If you have some kind of emotional issues—"

"I don't. I was physically injured and they're being picky about agents returning to the field at one hundred percent."

The truth was she wasn't sure she could go back and face the stares and whispers, sit for months, maybe years, behind a desk as agents paraded past with new cases.

"Max hired you at less than one hundred percent." He rested his head against the seat. "Interesting."

She'd better watch herself. If he was as smart as his reputation, she'd opened the door to his suspicions. Sure, she had an ulterior motive beyond finding the boy—she wanted to rebuild her reputation as an investigator and earn respect from her peers. She wanted to show Ivy that she could do anything, even excel in a man's world, if she put her mind to it.

"Government red tape kept me out of the field," she explained. "There's nothing wrong with me."

"I'm glad to hear it, because we're going to start by combing the beach for clues."

"The locals and feds have already done that." Her knee ached at the thought of marching on unstable sand.

"They might have missed something."

"I doubt it." She pulled in front of the Command Center and parked.

"Agent Ramos?" he said.

She glanced at him. Was that a smile playing across his lips?

"Yes?" she said.

"I'd be happy to find you a less strenuous position on the team."

Chapter Two

Tension arced across the room as the agents entered the Command Center. Neither Barnes nor Ramos are going to play well together in the proverbial sandbox.

Tough luck. Max knew he'd get the best from both of them if they worked together. Checks and balances. The determined female agent would keep a close watch on Barnes, maybe figure out what was going on with the man. He'd been off lately, distracted. Not at all like the consummate investigator Max had worked with at Scotland Yard. But Barnes's pride wouldn't allow him to admit vulnerability of any kind.

Max knew that feeling quite well.

He couldn't help but wonder if Barnes suffered from post-traumatic stress from nearly being blown to bits during their previous case. Jeremy was in complete denial that anything was wrong, yet he was just getting to work and it was the middle of the day.

They approached Max's office.

"Barnes, you're late." Max leaned back in his chair.

Theirs had always been a strained relationship, but after the last case Max actually felt a bit of kinship developing with his second in command.

"I'm not feeling well," Barnes said from the doorway.

Agent Ramos rolled her eyes.

Barnes slowly turned and looked through his rimless glasses at her. "Would you excuse us?"

With a lift of her chin she went to her desk.

Jeremy closed the office door and crossed his arms over his chest. "What the bloody hell were you thinking?"

"Excuse me?"

"That *female* does not belong here."

"You don't think so?" Max opened her file. "She's got five years with the federal government and seven years with local law enforcement."

Max also knew she was recovering from a bruised reputation. He could relate. She deserved a chance, much like the one Jeremy had given Max by asking him to lead the Blackwell Group.

He glanced at Jeremy. "She could be an asset to Blackwell if things work out. What's the trouble?"

"You mean besides the fact that she's argumentative and unprofessional?"

"Unprofessional?" Max chuckled.

"She broke into my room and was rifling through my things this morning."

Max glanced at his watch. "It's afternoon, mate, and I sent her because I was worried."

"I wasn't feeling well."

"So you said." Max eyed Barnes. Dark shadows circled beneath his bloodshot eyes. "Caught a bug, did you?"

"Seems like it."

It seemed more serious to Max. Did post-trauma terrors keep Barnes awake at night? Max had experienced the horror, the sweat-drenched anxiety attacks that would awaken him three or four times a night. It was the type of ailment you needed to tackle head on.

Max also knew firsthand about the devilish coping mechanism called denial. He'd buried his own struggle with post-traumatic stress the same way. Then Cassie came along and led him out of the darkness.

"Jeremy, Agent Ramos has recommendations from former supervisors and she seems like a determined young woman."

"Is that what you call it?"

Jeremy glanced into the main office at his new partner. She snapped her attention away from him and studied an open folder on her desk.

"You know I work alone," Jeremy said.

"You're my strongest investigator. I need you to train her to be a part of Blackwell."

"And then?" He glanced at Max.

"Then you're on your own. No partner required."

Jeremy nodded. "With any luck we'll solve this case as quickly as the last."

"I've left some new information on your desk. Look it over, will you? And ask Agent Ramos to step into my office."

Jeremy opened the office door, strode to Agent Ramos's desk and waited. It was a full five seconds before she looked up at him.

Bloody Nora, this woman was going to challenge Jeremy's self-control.

He said something to her then went to his desk. Ramos pulled her hair back into a ponytail and walked to Max's office.

"Close the door," he said.

Settling in a chair across the desk from him, she sat straight, at attention.

"When you first contacted me, you convinced me you'd be an asset to our team," Max started, hoping to resolve the tension.

"And Agent Barnes has convinced you otherwise?"

"Excuse me? I must admit I'm concerned about your attitude."

"I'm sorry, sir."

"Here's how it works. If you're a member of Blackwell, you're part of a team. A team only wins if all players work together."

"Did you give Agent Barnes this same lecture?"

"That's it, we're done."

Mercedes's heart slammed against her chest. "Done?"

Max leveled his steely green eyes at her. "We no longer require your services."

"But—"

"You pleaded with me to get on my team. I ignored rumors and took you at your word, assuming you were a professional with the determination I need from all of my agents. Instead, I get an argumentative woman who's looking for a fight around every corner. That, we don't need." He studied the newspaper in front of him.

Mercedes didn't know what to do. Sometimes her big mouth was her worst enemy.

"I'm sorry. I'm edgy because of my last case with the FBI. I'm used to being on the defensive, always having to prove myself." She paused. "I'd like to try again. Please?" She hated the sound of the word coming from her lips. Mercedes never begged or pleaded, not since the dark days under Papi's rule.

He glanced up. "That chip on your shoulder has already affected the team."

"Jeremy Barnes complained to you?"

"He doesn't have to. I can tell by the way the two of you interact that there's a problem."

"He's the problem. You should have seen him this morning." She tried to keep the judgment from her voice. "He could barely stand on his own two feet. His room was a mess, empty liquor bottles and food wrappers everywhere."

"Liquor bottles?"

"All empty. Look," she leaned forward in her chair. "I'm a good investigator. Don't ask me to babysit a drunk."

"He's not a drunk."

Great, another good old boys routine—protect your buddies, even if they're losers.

"Miss Ramos, I am in charge of Blackwell," Max said. "Jeremy is my second in command and a highly respected investigator. You should be honored that I paired you with him. I'm asking you to keep an eye on him, assist him with the Weddle investigation and report back to me. This means you'll have to work *with* him, not against him. Are you up to it?"

"Yes," she said without hesitation.

"You'll lose that chip on your shoulder?"

"Yes, sir." How on earth was she going to do that? Her resentment had fueled her drive to break out of the restrictive role females had in her culture. Her *chip* had become her best friend.

"Very well." He stood and, leaning heavily on his cane, went to the door.

She knew he'd been injured by a terrorist bombing in London and had read about his leave of absence. She wondered if his superiors had forced him out since he wasn't one hundred percent.

"Agent Barnes, please join us," Templeton said from the doorway.

Mercedes didn't miss the questioning glances from the other agents. She'd met Eddie Malone this morning, but the other two men were strangers.

A short blond woman breezed into the main office. The men greeted her with warm smiles. Who was she? Another investigator?

"Jeremy, Agent Ramos and I have come to an understanding," Max said.

Mercedes stood to gain equal footing in this conversation. Although she was nearly five eight, she felt much shorter than Barnes. She'd have to remember to wear her boots with the two-inch heels tomorrow.

"And what would that be?" Agent Barnes asked.

"I'm sorry if I made a bad impression," she said. "I drove all night from California to get here, so I'm a bit cranky."

"A bit?" Jeremy pushed.

"I said I was sorry." Sheesh, what did this guy want from her?

"Yes, you did," Max interjected. "Let's move on."

Clutching his brass-handled cane, Templeton led them into the main area. The cute little blonde glanced at him. Mercedes noticed his expression soften as he smiled in her direction.

Men could always be counted on to fall for a pretty face. Sure, Mercedes had been told how beautiful she was, but it meant nothing. She didn't want to use her natural beauty to get places in life.

Oh, you don't have to worry about that, chica. So far it has only worked against you.

"Quick catch-up," Templeton said. "Agent Barnes was feeling poorly this morning which is why he missed the briefing."

"Blimey, guv, you finally break down and go drinking?"

The group laughed at an inside joke made by the dark-haired man. Dark hair, dark eyes, a playful grin and a definite accent. Another Brit, Mercedes noted.

"Some of you met Agent Ramos this morning," Templeton started.

Mercedes felt naked standing there, four men and the woman eyeing her.

"She most recently worked with the FBI, before that Chicago PD. Agent Spinelli is also a former Chicago police officer."

A man nodded at her.

"Status of the Weddle case. The boy's been missing since Monday. We'll investigate four possibilities—accidental drowning, a search is still underway by the coast guard. Runaway, kidnapping or an Internet seduction. We've got access to a local forensics lab?"

"Working on it," Spinelli said.

"Good. Assignments are as follows—Eddie will

check family computers." Max looked at Barnes. "We'll need the boy's computer, which you can pick up when you interview friends and family in Mountain View."

"Yes, sir."

"Agent Finn, you're on Internet cafés in town, any place the boy could get online and talk to friends. Spinelli, get with local authorities to see how cooperative they are. Cassie will look into similar cases to this one. Barnes and Ramos, interview the parents, they're staying at Eagle Lodge, then meet me and Cassie at the beach near Eagle Rock."

"Are the Feds calling it an accidental drowning, guv?" Bobby asked.

"Not yet, but that's what we expect them to say by week's end. Susanna and Doug Weddle have hired us to find their son, dead or alive. I think he's still alive. In either event, he needs our help."

"Why do you think he's alive?" Mercedes asked.

"Instinct, Agent Ramos," her boss said, then turned back to the group. "Questions so far?"

Okay. They were all working on some guy's gut instinct here? What an odd group. Such trust, such loyalty.

She stifled the urge to point out that trusting one's gut was not the way most FBI cases were run.

Keep your mouth shut, chica. That's the only way they'll keep her on this team. This job will teach her self-control for sure.

"Here's what we know. The boy went missing on Monday. The bus left Eagle Rock Beach at one-thirty but they didn't notice him missing until they returned to school at 3 p.m. when the nanny came to pick him up. Everyone's got background in the folders, pertinent information about the family, friends and business associates. We'll reconvene at six."

They broke up and Spinelli approached her. He was a husky man in mid-thirties, wearing an American flag lapel pin.

"I was a detective with the Chicago PD. Which District did you work?" he said.

"The two-two."

"Homicide?"

"Started in patrol, then became a detective."

"Lucky girl."

He probably figured being female and a minority shot her right to the top of the detectives list. He wouldn't be the only one to assume as much. Didn't matter. She knew the truth. She'd studied endlessly and slept little in order to earn the top score on the exam.

"Hello, Miss," a man butted in. "Bobby Finn, at your service."

He shook her hand, a mischievous smile dimpling his cheek.

"Bobby," Max warned. "Behave."

"Don't I always, guv?" He winked at Mercedes. "I can't help it if women find me irresistible."

"Don't waste your time, Agent Finn," Barnes said, walking toward the door.

Jerk. Didn't he think her worthy of a little flirtation? Although she didn't encourage it, she didn't mind the attention. It's not like she'd let it go anywhere.

"Nice meeting you," she said to Bobby. She could use an ally.

Barnes disappeared outside and she raced after him feeling like a schoolgirl stalking her latest crush. She pushed through the door and caught up to him on the sidewalk. "We're not driving?"

"No. It's a beautiful day."

It was strange to hear a man appreciate the weather. But then, this was a very odd man.

He'd gone from sickly and weak, to confident and commanding in less than half an hour. He was hiding his hangover pretty well. Shoulders straight, head up, he walked with a casual, yet purposeful stride.

"Do you have a notebook?" he asked.

"I'm not your secretary."

He stopped and narrowed his guarded blue eyes at her. "I didn't say you were. I left mine in my hotel room."

Cripes, she'd done it again.

She had to let go of her paranoia if she wanted to make this work.

They continued toward the lodge. "What do we know about the parents?"

"They're transplants from Seattle. They moved to

Mountain View about a year ago. They were looking for a slower pace, a better life."

"And they lose a son."

She studied his long, narrow features, trying to figure out if she had heard remorse in his voice. She wondered if he was capable of expressing any kind of emotion then remembered his temper flaring this morning in his hotel room. He seemed the controlled type, the kind of man who would rather eat prunes than admit he had feelings, much less express them.

He'd been a hungover wreck when she'd found him. Then after his magical cup of tea, his entire demeanor had changed. She didn't know what to expect next. And she didn't like that feeling. It reminded her of walking on eggshells growing up, never knowing what kind of mood she'd have to deal with when Papi came home from work.

"What room number?" he asked.

She consulted her notebook. "Four twelve."

He held open the front door to Eagle Lodge.

"No, please." She motioned for him to enter first. She did not need a man taking care of her.

"As you wish." He entered and went to the elevator acting as if he could care less if she followed or not.

"You ever work with a partner before?" he said as they rode the elevator.

"Of course."

"What was the longest you stayed with one partner?"

"Two years, six months, fifteen days." *And a broken heart.*

Was that a smile curling the corner of his lips? Who could tell?

"And you?" she challenged.

"About three years."

The elevator doors opened and they both stepped inside, bumping arms.

"I'm sorry, I assumed you'd want to lead," he said in a wry tone.

A police officer stood outside the Weddles' room.

"I'm Jeremy Barnes, private investigator. This is my partner, Mercedes Ramos. We've been hired by the Weddle family to investigate their son's disappearance."

"The mother's inside. The father is at the beach with the task force," the officer said, eyeing Mercedes with obvious appreciation.

"Thank-you." Barnes knocked on the door and narrowed his eyes at the officer.

The man backed up an inch and cleared his throat. Mercedes looked from her partner to the local cop. What was this about? Barnes was acting as her protector? Not again.

The hotel room door opened. "Yes?" an elderly woman said.

"I'm Jeremy Barnes with the Blackwell Group. The Weddles hired us to find Lucas."

"Of course, come in."

She led them into a living area. "Wait here, I'll get my daughter."

Mercedes walked to the window and watched a team of investigators swarm the beach outside.

"I'll make introductions, you conduct the interview," Barnes said.

"You sure you trust me? After all, I'm your trainee." She struggled to keep the sarcasm from her voice. What was the deal here? Why did this particular man get under skin?

Because he was arrogant. Because he thought he was better than Mercedes.

"She will respond better to a compassionate woman than a questioning man," he said.

That took her by surprise, especially since he'd accused her of having the compassion of a serial killer earlier.

She studied this restrained man, his expressionless face and aristocratic profile. Was he thinking of the mother's tender emotions or the best way to solve the case?

She couldn't be sure. She thought she'd heard something resembling compassion in his deep, rich voice. Although his accent was strong, it was also very smooth and crisp, unlike Agent Finn's, which sounded choppy and hard.

The bedroom door opened and a short petite woman walked out, a cell phone to her ear.

"They just got here," she said. "Okay, I'll tell

them." She turned off the phone. "Hi, I'm Susanna Weddle." She shook hands with Mercedes first, then Jeremy. "That was my husband. He says to join him on the beach when we're done."

"Yes, ma'am," Mercedes said. "Are you up to a few questions?"

"Sure."

Mercedes noticed how the sofa practically swallowed the small woman as she sat down.

"Has your son been upset recently?" Mercedes started.

The woman grabbed a tissue.

Barnes shot Mercedes an odd look. What? He said to question her. Wait, right, he'd used the term *compassionate woman.*

"Why don't you tell us a little about Lucas." Mercedes tried again.

Mrs. Weddle cleared her throat. "He's bright, a bit shy, but trusting. He loves playing computer games."

"Does he play online?" Barnes interjected.

"Sometimes. But we monitor his activity very carefully."

"Does he like school?" Mercedes asked.

"He's homeschooled."

"But he went missing on a school trip?"

"He's taught at home, but he still goes on field trips through the school and participates in clubs."

"What sort of clubs?" Mercedes said.

"Science club, chess club, hiking club."

Mercedes jotted notes. Barnes crossed his arms over his chest and studied the woman.

"And your decision to homeschool him?" Mercedes continued.

"He's a smart boy. The public schools weren't challenging enough."

"Who were some of his friends?"

"His two close friends are Brad Reynolds and Shayne Lynk. We've been friends with the Lynks for years."

"We'll need their phone numbers."

"The Lynks are here in the lodge. They've been so supportive."

Mercedes smiled, then said, "Back to Lucas, was he looking forward to this field trip?"

"Very. He's never seen starfish before, or those little crabs that live along the beach. He wanted to study marine biology. Wants to study..." She blinked back a tear and Mercedes's heart ached for her.

She eyed Barnes. His expression hadn't changed.

Mrs. Weddle leveled a gaze at Mercedes. "He's a good swimmer."

Mercedes studied her notebook to avoid the woman's pain. "And you didn't notice any change in his behavior recently? Moodiness? Anything like that?"

"Don't."

Mercedes glanced up. “Excuse me?”

“Don’t act like the police. I’m sick of their questions and insinuations.”

“Insinuations?” Barnes repeated.

“They think it’s our fault that he’s gone.”

It made sense she’d get that impression. Family usually topped the suspect list in criminal cases.

“I’m sure even routine questions can sound offensive at a time like this,” Mercedes said.

“Excuse me.” Barnes paced to the sliding glass doors overlooking the beach and answered his cell phone.

“Do *you* think it’s my fault?”

Mercedes snapped her attention to the woman, whose eyes misted over with tears.

“You could not have known that this would happen,” Mercedes said.

“Are you a mother, Miss Ramos?”

“No.” Her heart ached. She’d been so busy with her career she hadn’t had time to think about a family of her own.

Mrs. Weddle stared blankly at the coffee table. Mercedes wanted to comfort her, but didn’t know how. Her goal in life had been to prove herself in a man’s world. She wasn’t sure she had a nurturing side although Mami said it would come when she had children. *That* wasn’t happening any time soon. Not until she found a man who could respect her as an equal.

"Mrs. Weddle." Barnes stepped toward them. "They've found something."

Chapter Three

Jeremy and Mercedes accompanied Mrs. Weddle to the beach. As they stepped onto the cool sand, Jeremy spotted her husband in the distance speaking with a Coast Guard officer.

"Oh, God," Mrs. Weddle said, hesitating.

It was then he noticed that a second officer was holding a clear plastic bag with a red-and-blue backpack inside.

"Lu-cas!" she cried, racing toward her husband.

Her husband caught her as her legs gave out. She sobbed against his chest.

Jeremy gently touched Mercedes's shoulder. "Let's give them a moment." She glanced at his hand and he thought she might give him a lecture on sexual harassment.

But he hadn't touched her that way.

He could see how any warm-blooded man would be tempted to cross that line. Although she was dressed conservatively in black trousers, a gray blouse and black jacket, it was obvious she hid a shapely figure beneath the loose cut of her suit.

He wasn't the only one who'd noticed. First Bobby had flirted with her, then the cop guarding the Weddle's hotel room had practically accosted her in the hallway. She was beautiful, to be sure, but was she a sharp investigator?

He didn't care about her model-type looks or wary expression. For a tough girl she was easy to read, at least for Jeremy. He read pain, disappointment and a fighting spirit in her eyes. The spirit intrigued him.

No, he needed to focus on training her so she could partner with someone else. Who knows, maybe Bobby would get lucky and draw her number.

Jeremy chuckled inside at the image of Bobby being paired with Mercedes. She was a lot more complicated than the typical females Bobby attracted.

Beautiful and complicated. Jeremy had done beautiful and complicated once. He ended up with a broken heart and a cynical nature. It was the only time he'd considered himself a fool. Never again.

Doug Weddle motioned for Jeremy to join him. "Mister?"

"Agent Barnes, and this is Agent Ramos."

"So, you've got something?" he said, expectant.

"The team's in the process of setting up, sir. We'll need to familiarize ourselves with the case before we can draw any conclusions."

"And when will that be? Next week?"

Jeremy held steady, not allowing himself to be drawn into this man's emotional tornado. He obviously loved his son very much. An ache started low in Jeremy's gut.

"We're running out of time here and you're doing nothing," Mr. Weddle accused.

Mercedes planted her hands to her hips. "That's not entirely true, sir."

"Was it your son's backpack?" Jeremy interrupted. He'd have to speak with her about keeping her feelings to herself and not getting offended by a father's natural reaction to a lost child.

Mr. Weddle watched the Coast Guard officers walk toward a Jeep with the bag. "Yes, it's Lucas's."

"He never would have left it," Mrs. Weddle said. "He keeps his notebook in there, the one with all his experiments."

"What kind of experiments?" Jeremy pushed.

"Science experiments," the father said, one arm around his wife, while running the other hand through thick brown hair. "Burning leaves by using a magnifying glass, growing plants indoors using fluorescent lights—stuff like that."

"Where did they find the backpack?" Jeremy asked.

"About a half mile out. The dive team found it."

"Was anything missing?"

"We're not sure. They want us to come down to their office to open it."

"My mobile number." Jeremy handed him a card. "We'll be in the lodge interviewing the Lynks. Meet us there when you're finished."

"Sure, okay."

Jeremy nodded and started toward the shoreline. He'd spotted Max and Cassie in the distance and was anxious to get Max's take on this case. It didn't seem like an accidental drowning. The dive team should have found the body by now.

Thank goodness they hadn't. The thought of another lost boy tore at his heart.

"Weddle's got high expectations. We've only been on this case a day," Mercedes said.

"How did you expect him to respond? His child's gone missing, everyone around him assumes the boy's dead and he can't do anything about it." He glanced at her. "This isn't about us not doing our job. It's about a father having his heart ripped out. Shelve the ego, Agent Barnes."

"Whoa, this seems awfully personal to you all of the sudden."

It was. It was about a lost boy. Like Phillip.

This case was getting to him. Or, was it this female?

"We may be partners, but you take direction from me," he said. "Focus on the boy or on the mother who's lost her child. Not on the grieving father's critical comments. Are we clear?"

Her eyes blazed fire and her cheeks reddened.

She nodded, probably unable to speak unless to utter a curse word.

Too bad. She had a beautiful voice, her words flavored by her accent. Beautiful woman, beautiful voice and self-absorbed. But it said nothing about her potential as an investigator.

It had been years since he'd thought about a woman as anything but a work associate. Sure, there had been a roll in the hay here and there, but nothing that resembled a relationship.

Not that he'd recognize one of those. After his father had left, Mum rarely interacted with Jeremy except to criticize. That's when he'd learned to control his emotions, keep them strapped down tight. She did her worst when he opened himself up to her by sharing his feelings and fears.

Stop your crying, you puffer. Be a man.

The only attention he got from his father was when Jeremy agreed to pursue a career in law. Father and son time was spent at the club, his father impressing his friends with Jeremy's grade point average.

Jeremy realized he'd probably been a mistake. He accepted that fact, stopped trying to please them and followed his heart—he wanted to be a police inspector.

They'd disowned him, but he didn't care. He couldn't miss what he'd never had.

Although Templeton and blokes like him thought

Jeremy hoity-toity, he'd worked his way through university after his father had cut him off. He wasn't the spoiled prince they made him out to be. But he let them think what they liked. It taught him a valuable lesson—people were not what they appeared to be.

They approached Max and Cassie. Cute girl, she was exactly what she appeared to be—lively, open and caring. Max was a lucky bastard. She'd seen him at his worst, yet still wanted to spend the rest of her life with him.

Jeremy didn't fool himself into thinking he'd be so lucky.

"What did they find?" Max inquired, squinting against the midday sunshine.

"The boy's backpack," Jeremy said. "The divers found it about a mile from shore."

Max glanced toward the ocean.

"That supports the drowning theory," Jeremy said.

"It does, doesn't it?"

Jeremy heard the doubt in his voice. "Something's bothering you, guv?"

"Not sure yet." He glanced at Jeremy. "How did the interviews go?"

"We only spoke with the mother," Mercedes offered. "We were interrupted by the backpack development."

"Did you get names of friends and schoolmates?"

"The boy was homeschooled, but we have

names and phones numbers of two family friends," Barnes said.

"Good. Walk with us." Max motioned for Jeremy to keep pace beside him.

Mercedes was a little uncomfortable beside the blond woman, but wasn't sure why.

"I'm Cassie Clarke. I meant to welcome you earlier."

Mercedes shook her hand. "Thanks. What department are you from?"

"Department? Oh, you mean police. No, I'm Mr. Templeton's assistant. If you have any questions or need anything, feel free to ask," Cassie said.

"Thanks."

The woman acted like she enjoyed the role of Max's assistant and she seemed genuinely kind. Mercedes wasn't sure how to handle that since she was used to being on the defensive.

"What made you decide to come on board?" Cassie asked.

"I was on leave from the FBI and was bored out of my mind. I heard about Blackwell from an agent named Curtis Sykes."

Curtis, a forensic psychologist, had been her mentor and had never tried to hit on her. She glanced at the back of her new partner. She wouldn't have to worry about Cold Barnes hitting on her, that's for sure.

"I heard Agent Sykes is going to consult from Michigan," Cassie said.

"Seems cut-and-dried to me. They found his backpack in the ocean. The boy drowned."

"Oh, no," Cassie said, touching Mercedes's arm. "We've got to be positive."

The woman's lack of law enforcement experience was apparent. She'd probably been sheltered her whole life and had never seen the ugliness of violent crime.

"This is where he was last seen." Templeton pointed toward a large rock that protruded out from the ocean. It must have been two hundred feet high.

"The teachers were having the students look for starfish and puffins," Templeton added. "Since it was an afternoon visit, the tide was too high to allow students access to the rock. In the morning you can walk straight out and touch it, although they discourage such proximity to protect the wildlife. Right, well, the police theory is that the boy, being fascinated with science and nature, broke away from the group and waded into the water, lost his footing and went under."

"The mother said he's a good swimmer," Mercedes offered.

"But the backpack could have weighed him down," Barnes countered.

"Then the tide swept him out to sea? Something doesn't tally." Templeton scanned the horizon.

"What are you thinking, guv?" Barnes said.

"The local police and Coast Guard are working

on the theory that the boy drowned. Let's focus on the possibility that he's alive."

"You mean he ran away?" Barnes asked.

"That's one option." Templeton eyed the large rock protruding from the ocean. "Find out how things were with his parents recently. Boys can be a handful."

"But his mother said he was a good boy, he's into science and computer games, not the kind of kid that would run away," Mercedes added.

"Did you keep secrets from your mother, Agent Ramos?"

She didn't expect that question. An image of sneaking out to dance with Antonio flashed across her thoughts. Jeremy caught her eye and she glanced at the sand.

"We all did." Max shot her a knowing smile. "A mother's impression is one-sided. Talk to the Lynks. Then drive out to Mountain View and speak to the boy's sister and friends. Bring Lucas's computer back with you. The police shouldn't object since they're so close to calling it an accidental drowning. Maybe Lucas shared secrets with friends over the Internet."

"Yes, sir." Barnes took a step on the sand and wavered, then steadied himself.

"You all right there, Barnes?" Templeton asked.

"Fine. We'll check in later." He started for the hotel. "Let's get that interview out of the way."

"I've got a better idea," she said.

He eyed her.

"Let's get some food in you."

"I'm fine."

"You almost fell over. You're going to eat. If there's one thing I know how to do it's take care of a partner with a hangover."

"I do not have a hangover."

Wasn't that what they all said, starting with Papi? The only way to live with him the morning after was to make strong coffee, as only Mercedes could, and give him peace and quiet.

Then there was Fitzsimmons, her senior officer in Chicago for six months. He'd show up at work irritable and hung over and she'd automatically fetch his coffee, resenting the fact that she was taking care of yet another man.

They went to Eagle Lodge and found the Lynks in the coffee shop.

"Good. Now maybe you'll eat something," she said.

"Why the concern about my health?"

Barnes would flip if he knew she'd been assigned to watch over him.

"I don't want you slowing us down because you have low blood sugar."

She spotted the Lynks at a table by the window and picked up her pace.

"Mr. Lynk, we're with the Blackwell Group," she

said. "I'm Mercedes Ramos and this is Jeremy Barnes."

"Yes, of course." He stood. "Please join us."

They did, and Mercedes flagged the waitress, a twentyish girl with red hair. "What's the soup today?"

"Chicken rice or split pea."

"Bring him a bowl of chicken soup, mostly broth, dry toast and a glass of orange juice. I'll have coffee."

"Yes, ma'am."

Jeremy shot her a look probably meant to scold her.

She smiled at him, then turned to Mr. Lynk. "Your son was friends with Lucas?"

She pulled her notebook from her suit jacket pocket.

"Yes, close friends, although they were a year apart in school."

"Your son attended public school?"

"Private, actually. The Mercer Academy."

"How often did your son and Lucas get together?"

"Once, twice a week," the wife said. She picked at a half eaten salad. "They had play dates. Plus, we belonged to a fantasy investment club with the Weddles. We met every month."

"Fantasy?"

"It was an excuse to get together," Mr. Lynk said. "There was no real money involved."

"And children were invited to your meetings?"

"Sometimes they came and watched movies or played video games."

"We'll need names and phone numbers of club members."

"You don't think this has anything to do with the club?" Mr. Lynk said.

"No, sir. But it would help to speak with anyone who has been around Lucas recently to get an idea of his state of mind."

"My address book is up in the room," Mrs. Lynk said. "I'll leave the information at the front desk."

The waiter delivered soup, toast and juice. Jeremy stared at it as if it were a live squid. His stomach must feel like hell.

"Where is your son now?" Mercedes asked the mother.

"My parents are staying with him at the house."

"I didn't think it would be a good idea to bring him along in case…" The father's voice trailed off and he stared into his coffee.

She knew what he was going to say—in case they found the dead body of Lucas Weddle. It was a definite possibility, even if members of the Blackwell Group were determined otherwise.

"How did you meet the Weddles?" Mercedes asked.

"We were business associates for years," Mr. Lynk offered. "I'm a marketing consultant and he hired me to promote his new line of software. It really took off. Anyway, when he sold the company he became an instant millionaire. He grew a little jaded after getting the screws put to him by family and so-called friends wanting handouts. I kept in touch, but I didn't want anything from him. I thought he was an interesting guy. Then our wives became friends."

Mr. Lynk glanced over Mercedes's shoulder. "There's Paul. Paul, over here," he called.

Mercedes glanced across the restaurant. A tall, thin man, maybe forty, with a receding hairline joined them.

"This is Paul Reynolds, a family friend," Mr. Lynk said. "These are the investigators hired to find Lucas."

They shook hands.

"Any news?" he asked Jeremy.

"They found the boy's backpack in the ocean," Mercedes offered.

"God, no," Mrs. Lynk said.

They shared a moment of contemplative silence.

"But no sign of Lucas?" Reynolds said, hope in his voice.

"Not yet," Jeremy offered.

"Paul, join us for lunch," Mr. Lynk said.

"Thanks, but, I've got business in town buying some property. I just thought I'd stop by and check on the progress. Where are Doug and Susanna?"

"With the task force," Mercedes said.

"Oh, right," he said, somewhat distracted. "Well, nice meeting you." He nodded and left the restaurant.

"Mr. Reynolds is part of this investment club?" Jeremy asked.

"Yes, he and his wife, Ann," Mr. Lynk said. "They've actually invested real money in club stock and have done pretty well. Wish I could say the same."

Mercedes glanced at Jeremy's plate. He hadn't touched it. She inched it closer to him.

"A few more questions," she said. "How were things between Mr. and Mrs. Weddle lately?"

"Excuse me?" Mr. Lynk leaned back in his chair.

"These are routine questions," Barnes explained. "We're trying to understand the family dynamics."

"Doug and Susanna are very happy." The man glared at Mercedes.

Ay carumba, she'd stepped into it again.

"When was the last time you saw the Weddles?" Mercedes asked.

"About two weeks ago," Mr. Lynk said. "The Reynolds had a barbecue and invited our family, Doug, Susanna and Lucas and another family that has a son about Lucas's age. They were neighbors of the Reynolds."

"Lucas seemed okay?" Mercedes asked. "Not worried or bothered by anything?"

"No."

"Mrs. Lynk?" Barnes said.

"Hmm?" She glanced up.

"Everything seemed okay to you?"

"Yes, fine." She shot Mercedes a strained smile.

Then, maybe that was a normal smile for the woman.

"If you think of anything that could be helpful, here's my number." Barnes handed Mr. Lynk a business card, then stood and shook his hand. "We're heading to Mountain View this afternoon. May I have your permission to speak with your son?"

Mr. Lynk eyed Mercedes. "If you can manage not to upset him."

"We're trying to keep his hopes up by telling him Lucas got lost in one of the caves or something," Mrs. Lynk said. "But I'm sure he hears the worry in our voices."

"Of course," Barnes said. "Thank-you for your time."

"Eh, eh," Mercedes said. "Your lunch. I'll have them box it for you."

She motioned for the waitress who brought their check and a to-go container.

Barnes took the check. "I'll meet you up front."

Feeling like Barnes's mother, Mercedes boxed the toast, nodded at the Lynks and hooked up with him by the register.

"I need to speak to my waitress," he said.

"Okay." The hostess went into the back.

"Hey, it's not her fault you didn't feel like eating," Mercedes said.

He ignored her.

"Stop acting like I'm invisible."

Nothing. Old frustrations tangled with her common sense. "You're being rude," she said.

"And you weren't when you insinuated the Weddles were having marital problems?"

"I didn't insinuate—"

"It's the way you asked the question. Do you have to be so direct?"

"Ask a direct question—get a direct answer. It's my style and it's always worked for me."

He narrowed his eyes at her.

Okay, maybe not always.

Their waitress approached. "Was there a problem, sir?"

"Did you write this?" He flipped over the check and Mercedes noticed scribbles on the back.

"No," the waitress said.

"Who had access to your order pad?"

"The cook, anyone in back, I guess."

"Show me."

The waitress led them into the kitchen, past grills, refrigerators and sanitizing sinks.

"What's through there?" He pointed toward a door.

"That leads out back."

"Thank you." He pushed open the door and went outside.

Mercedes followed him to the break area—a cement patio with a picnic table. Barnes followed a stone path that led to a split-rail fence and a spectacular view of the ocean.

"Are you going to clue me in here, boss?" Mercedes said.

Without looking at her, he handed her the order ticket. She flipped it over. The words *abandoned, lost* and *betrayed* were scribbled across the paper at least a dozen times.

"What does that mean?" she said.

He stared her down, the intensity of his sky blue eyes disarming. "I'm wondering why the Weddles haven't received a ransom demand. Or have they?"

Chapter Four

They waited in the lobby for the Weddles to return from going through Lucas's backpack. Jeremy hoped he was wrong, hoped the parents weren't playing both sides by pretending there had been no ransom request.

But it wouldn't surprise him. A powerful man like Doug Weddle probably feared the authorities would muddle the ransom drop, causing him to lose his son.

Besides, when you had money it was easier to take care of things yourself. Isn't that how Father always handled it? Buy his way out of a marriage; buy his way out of fatherhood. Easy enough.

"You sure you're up to this?" she asked.

"Meaning?"

"You didn't eat your lunch."

"I'm not hungry."

"Ah, you and your macho thing." She stood. "I'll get you a Gatorade."

"I don't need..." His voice trailed off as he watched her walk through the lobby and disappear around a corner.

Was she trying to earn points with him by playing concerned partner? Or was she looking for an excuse to get away from him? That was probably it. Their energy was like wind and water—she was all over the place and he was calm and controlled. It must drive her crazy to be around such a composed man. She wouldn't be the first. Collegues found Jeremy's nature disarming and unpleasant at times. Even his longest partner, Smitty, used to taunt Jeremy to get a reaction.

But Jeremy's reserved nature was his protection, his strength.

He scanned the lobby, waiting for Mercedes to round the corner. She was probably trying to get on his good side to earn a permanent place on the team.

Fine, as long as it wasn't as his partner. Her frenetic energy distracted him, made it hard to think. Or was it something else that distracted him? Those big brown eyes, perhaps?

"Mr. Barnes?" the hotel receptionist called across the small rustic lobby.

"Yes?" He walked to the front desk.

"This was dropped off a minute ago." She handed him an envelope.

Probably contact names and numbers from Mrs. Lynk.

"Thank you." He opened the envelope and pulled out a photocopy of a newspaper clipping, "Officers Shot in Drug Deal Gone Bad."

His heart slammed against his chest. Beneath the headline was a photograph of Jeremy and Smitty taken ten years ago. What in the bloody hell was this about? No one knew about that case except for Templeton and he had no reason to taunt Jeremy.

Across the top of the clipping someone had written,

How r u feeling, Inspector?

Meaning what? Whoever sent the clipping knew that he'd been ill this morning? Or worse, this person caused Jeremy's illness?

His well-ordered life unraveled at his feet. "Who gave this to you?"

"Freddie from maintenance said some guy from Blackwell dropped it off."

Which made no sense. No, someone must have been pretending to be with the team. Who would go to all this trouble to torment Jeremy? He mentally listed off felons he'd put away, but to his knowledge they were back in London.

"Interesting reading?" Ramos said, smacking an energy drink to the front desk.

"No, nothing." He folded the newspaper clipping and shoved it into his pocket. He didn't need his partner or anyone else knowing about this, not when he didn't know what to make of it himself. He didn't want to distract the team from their current case.

He'd let a boy down once before. He wouldn't let it happen again.

"You okay? You look worse than when I found you this morning." She eyed him.

"I'm fine."

"You're dehydrated." She slid the energy drink in front of him.

He could argue with her, but it seemed easier to drink the yellow-green liquid. His mind spun like a slot machine, trying to land on the identity of his tormentor.

He spotted the Weddles entering the lodge.

"I'll handle this," she said. "You don't look so good."

Of course not. An unknown stalker had threatened him during a critical missing persons investigation.

"Besides," Mercedes added, "I seem to be a natural at the bad cop role." She shot him a smile and glanced at the couple.

"How did it go, Mr. Weddle?" Mercedes asked, motioning for them to join her and Jeremy in the lobby.

The husband led his wife to a sofa and they sat down.

"We went through Lucas's backpack," Mr.

Weddle said. "I'm not sure what's missing. God…" He ran an open palm across his face. "I don't even know what he keeps in his backpack."

"His compass," the mother said, staring off into space. "He always has a compass with him."

"Mr. Weddle, I need to ask you a few questions, okay?" Mercedes said.

Jeremy was relieved that she'd elbowed her way into the role of lead interviewer. He needed a few minutes to get his focus back. Had the note from the restaurant been for Mr. Weddle or Jeremy? He'd have to show it to Templeton. Mercedes knew about it. There was no pretending it didn't exist.

But Jeremy wouldn't allow it to be a distraction. He was a master at compartmentalizing his feelings. For now, he'd shove this personal attack into a chamber and lock it up so he could focus on finding the boy.

"Anything unusual happen in your family during the past few weeks?" Mercedes started.

"Unusual?"

"Odd visitors to the house, strange mail or e-mail threats?"

"No, nothing like that," Mr. Weddle said. "Why aren't you out there looking for my son?"

"The local authorities and Coast Guard are on top of the search," she said. "We want to try a different angle."

"What angle?"

"The possibility that he was abducted."

Jeremy studied Doug Weddle's expression. It transformed from anger to relief at the suggestion that his son was still alive. Or was it relief that his secret had been found out? That he didn't have to hide the ransom demand?

"Has anyone been in contact with you, sir?" Jeremy tried.

"God, no. Don't you think I would have told you?"

"Of course." Mercedes shot Jeremy a perturbed look, then turned back to Mr. Weddle. "How has Lucas been acting lately?"

"Good. Fine. He's ten. He's going through some things."

"What kinds of things?"

"He's fighting a lot with his sister," Mrs. Weddle said. "She's four and wants all the attention. She'll break things to get it if she has to."

"Lucas's things?"

"Yes."

"Which means what?" Doug Weddle said. "That he ran away because his sister broke his toy tower?"

"It was more than a toy to him," the mother said. "It was an exact replica of your building in downtown Seattle, Doug."

"He wouldn't have run away because she destroyed it. That's absurd," the father argued.

"Mr. Weddle, we're not casting judgment or making accusations," Jeremy said. "We're trying to get a sense of what was going on in his life at the time of the disappearance."

"Nothing was going on. He's a typical ten-year-old."

"He's not typical," the mother whispered.

"You know what I meant." He hugged her.

"He's smart. Like you," she whispered. "He always admired you so."

"Don't talk like that. He's not gone. He's just lost."

"And we're here to find him," Jeremy interrupted before they went too far down that road. "We're headed to Mountain View to interview Shayne Lynk. With your permission we'd like to bring your son's computer back with us."

"Sure," Doug Weddle said. "My parents are staying at the house with Natalia."

"Would you mind if we spoke with her?" Jeremy asked.

"She's only four," the father protested. "Okay, fine. Whatever you need to do, do it."

"Thank-you." Jeremy and Mercedes left and headed back to the Command Center.

"So, you still think they received a ransom demand?" Mercedes said.

Jeremy considered Doug Weddle's expression of relief. "Hard to tell. We gave him the perfect opportunity to come clean."

"And he didn't take it. I don't think he's hiding anything."

"You can never be too sure. People are often not what they appear to be."

"Aren't you the cynical one?"

"I'm also wondering about the scribblings on the order pad."

"Wondering what?"

"If it has anything to do with this case, or if it was just scribblings."

He ignored her expression of disbelief.

"Of course it's related to this case. What else could it be?"

Abandoned. Lost. Betrayed. Was it a message from Jeremy's stalker or the person responsible for Lucas's disappearance?

"I've been thinking about those words," he said. "The boy is lost, but how could he be abandoned and betrayed?"

"We find that out and it might lead us to Lucas," she said. "I'm thinking personal enemies. Someone who thought Doug Weddle shafted him in business. Let's drop that note off at the Command Center. Maybe they can find fingerprints besides yours and the waitress's."

They left the note with Spinelli, who was going to take it to a forensics lab. Max and Cassie hadn't returned from the beach. Just as well, Barnes couldn't risk Max figuring out something was bothering his second in command. Max had a keen sense about people, especially Jeremy.

Luckily, Agent Ramos didn't have that same talent, at least not where Jeremy was concerned.

She insisted on driving, saying he needed to focus on eating his lunch. When they picked up sandwiches, he felt like a twit for only having two dollars left in his wallet. Last night he could have sworn he'd had close to fifty dollars.

"I'll get this one," she said with a smile, as if she enjoyed the thought of him owing her.

She unwrapped his sandwich, handed it to him like an overprotective mother and headed out of town. He eyed her as she sipped her cola.

"You come from a large family?" He took a bite of his sandwich.

"Four kids—two boys, two girls. You?"

He swallowed. "Just me."

"Ah, that explains it," she said, pulling onto the highway.

"What?"

"The way you are. You seem uncomfortable around people."

"Maybe I'm just uncomfortable around you."

She narrowed her eyes at him. "Why?"

"Drop the female-racist thing, will you?"

"Who says I was thinking that?"

"You've been thinking that ever since you joined the team. But if it works for you..."

"Yeah, you think you know me, British?"

"Now who's racist?"

That shut her up. But he didn't want her quiet, he wanted her talking, scolding, arguing; anything to keep his mind off this strange turn of events.

How r u feeling, Inspector?

"Why police work?" he asked her to distract himself.

"Why not?" she countered.

He shook his head.

"What?" She glanced at him, then back at the road.

"Everything I say, you interpret as an insult."

"That's not true."

"Why a career in law enforcement then?" He took another bite of his sandwich.

"Because I like catching bad guys."

"And?"

"And what?"

"Everyone wants to catch criminals. There's usually something else involved, something personal."

"Yeah? You first. What personal thing made you want to be a cop?"

"I wanted to catch *bad guys.*" He smiled.

"And?" she challenged.

"Being a police officer royally upset my parents."

"I know *that* feeling. Mami says I should be home with four children by now." She brushed crumbs off her black pants.

"How old are you, if you don't mind me asking?"

"Thirty-one."

"Four kids?"

"She'd had hers by the time she turned thirty."

"But the mommy thing isn't for you?"

"Maybe, someday, after I have a successful career. I'm trying to set an example for my little sister. Show her she has options. Why didn't your parents want you to be a cop?"

"They wanted me to be a lawyer."

She grimaced.

"I agree," he said. "They expected me to follow in my father's footsteps, study law, join his firm and bill wealthy clients for thousands of pounds."

"Your family is wealthy?"

"Relatively." Not that he would see any of the family fortune.

She placed the remainder of her sandwich back in the wrapper. "If my family was wealthy, I wouldn't be working so hard."

He smiled. "Yes, you would."

"You think you know me?"

"Ah, on the defensive again," he joked. Maybe if he kept this mindless banter going he'd calm the panic filling his chest.

"The defensive is natural for me," she said. "I've had to fight for everything."

Unlike you, he heard. Just like the rest, she assumed Jeremy the spoiled type.

"For instance?" he prompted.

"My jobs. I have to prove myself over and over again."

"Prove yourself?"

"Yes. Prove that it's not my sex or my race that gets me promotions."

"Reverse discrimination, you mean?"

"Sure. I'm a female Latina. It looks good to have a double minority on the payroll."

"You really believe that? That your race opens doors for you?"

"It's what the rest of the world thinks."

Interesting. The girl was trying to prove something to the faceless mass of humanity. That was a tall order.

They drove a few minutes in silence, Jeremy welcoming the peace of a quiet country road. It was a gorgeous coastal drive.

"So, where will we go first?" she said, eyeing a sign that read, Mountain View—Ten Miles.

Did the silence bother her? He'd grown used to it over the years, welcomed it over the alternative—his mother's rantings.

"I'd like to speak with Lucas's friend, Shayne, then head over to the Weddles' house and interview the sister and pick up Lucas's computer. Eddie's a talented bloke with those things."

"I'll have to check out this Eddie a little more closely," she joked.

It felt odd, her joking, Jeremy talking. This was the most he'd spoken to a coworker in years. He'd given orders and discussed theories, but rarely did he converse about anything other than the case at hand.

It was even more odd that he'd strike up a conversation with Mercedes, a passionate woman who seemed unafraid of exposing her thoughts and feelings.

Dangerous indeed.

She glanced in the rearview. "What's this guy's problem?"

He looked out the back window. A truck was following so close he couldn't see the headlights.

"The bloke's obviously in a rush."

She muttered a curse in Spanish.

"Don't take it personally," he said. "If he's in a hurry, he'd be on anybody's tail. We just happened to be ahead of him."

"How can you be so calm?"

"What good will it do to get angry? Why don't you pull over and let him pass."

"No, the jerk can pull around us."

"It's a competition then?"

"Very funny," she said.

A bump jerked them forward. "Bastard!" she cried. "He hit us."

"Pull over."

"We need to get his plate number."

"Just pull over and let him pass."

He dug his fingers into the dash realizing this could be more than a motorist in a hurry. Was it his stalker?

"Pull over now!"

She ignored him and studied the rearview mirror. "I'm gonna nail that jerk. Can you get a good look at him?"

"Forget about that lunatic. Let him pass. That's an order, Agent Ramos."

She glared at him. Then turned on her blinker.

The truck edged closer. Blast, who was this bastard?

"Back off!" she said.

The truck jerked forward and hit their back bumper, shoving them toward the cliff overlooking the ocean.

Jeremy's head whipped back and Mercedes spun the wheel.

He gripped the dash, adrenaline pumping through his body as the car jerked to a stop a few feet from the overlook.

"The jerk doesn't even have a back license plate!" she cried.

He took a calming breath. Of course he didn't have a back plate—driving like that, he wouldn't want to be identified.

Jeremy got out of the car and took a deep breath. The truck was nothing but two spots of red taillights in the distance. He went to the back of the car and noticed a dent in the bumper.

It could have been much worse. They could have landed in the ocean.

Mercedes got out and waved a fist in the truck's

direction. "Can you believe that guy? What was he trying to do, kill us?"

Her long black ponytail swung to the front as she carried on, waving her hands and cursing in Spanish. She wore her emotions on her sleeve, whereas Jeremy hid them deep in his heart. She was a wild one and sexy as hell when angry.

What are you thinking, Barnes? You could have been killed just now. Mercedes could have been killed. She didn't deserve to be in danger because of Jeremy. Was the truck related to the threat he'd received? Or was it a coincidence?

No, Jeremy didn't believe that. He had to convince Templeton to assign Mercedes a new partner as soon as they returned from Mountain View. Which meant he had to tell Templeton about the newspaper clipping.

Jeremy eyed the highway where the truck had disappeared. "He was in a hurry, for sure."

"A hurry? That's all you have to say? He was in a hurry? He's dangerous. Probably drunk. We'll report that jerk when we hit the next town."

"We don't have time to stop. Let's keep moving. I'll drive."

Mercedes watched him get back in the car, calm and collected. He wasn't rattled in the least about nearly being killed by psycho driver.

Did the man feel *anything?*

She got in the car and they pulled away.

"I can do the interviews if you're too shaken," he said.

"You should be shaken, too. What's the matter with you?"

"I'm sorry?"

"All this control. A man just tried to kill us and you, you're nothing."

"You know it was a man because a woman wouldn't drive like that?"

"Jokes? How can you joke about this?"

He opened and closed his fingers around the steering wheel. Okay, so he was feeling something.

Maybe he was being a gentleman, acting calm for her benefit. She'd heard about men doing that but had never experienced it firsthand.

Or maybe he was—a passionless detective who didn't let anything get to him.

What a sad way to live your life.

"I'm fine." She stared out the window, cursing herself for losing it. She couldn't help it. She hated stupidity and that driver was number one stupid.

Which made her partner what? She'd given him that title up to now, considered him a drunken fool. After all, one minute he thought the words written on the check were a lead, the next he dismissed them. He was completely inconsistent.

Plus the man was more than a bit secretive. He was keeping something from her. That piece of paper he'd shoved into his pocket at the lodge had turned his face white. Maybe they'd revoked his VISA. She smiled at that one. The supposedly brilliant, but bumbling Brit being shipped back to England.

Yet before, when they were chatting, he'd seemed natural and honest. She eyed him. Yes, she could see him as an attorney, not a cop. With that reserved control he could prosecute and convict criminals, using facts and evidence as his road map. She imagined that same control could drive him mad if he kept the ugliness of his job bottled up inside.

He seemed too sophisticated to be a cop, not the type to get his hands dirty. That's why he had Mercedes around, to take notes, ask questions and buy him lunch.

"Hey, I want to be reimbursed for your tuna sandwich."

He cracked a smile. Odd, how that subtle expression changed his face completely. He went from cold, disinterested detective to intriguing man; a man with intense blue eyes that fascinated her.

Forget it, chica.

She hadn't seen it coming with her last partner; but she'd be walking straight into the fire if she found herself the least bit interested in Jeremy Barnes as anything other than a way to solidify her position with Blackwell.

She glanced at the trees that whizzed by as they headed to Mountain View. Mercedes pushed all thoughts of this puzzling man out of her mind and focused on her interviews—a four-year-old sister, a ten-year-old friend; so young to be dealing with this kind of tragedy.

Then again, she shouldn't assume the boy had drowned. What had that girl Cassie said? *We've got to be positive.*

A foreign concept for Mercedes.

"What's this about?" Barnes said, as they approached town.

Her stomach clenched at the sight of flashing blue lights. Three squad cars were in place, officers stopping and speaking to motorists. Barnes lowered his window.

"Officer?" he said. "We're with the Lucas Weddle investigation. What's happened?"

"Lucas's sister is missing."

Chapter Five

"We're pulling over cars to ask if anyone's seen her and to make sure she hasn't been abducted," the officer said.

Mercedes's chest ached. First the son disappears, now the daughter? What had the Weddles done to deserve this horror?

She thought about the note—*abandoned, lost, betrayed.*

"We're expected at the Weddle house," Barnes said to the officer.

"Take a right at the second stop sign and follow it about a mile. The girl's been missing less than an hour."

"Who reported her missing?"

"The grandmother. She's pretty shook up."

"Thanks. Oh, I don't suppose anyone reported a red truck racing through town in the last half hour?"

"No, sir, why? Does it have something to do with the missing girl?"

"It ran us off the road and it didn't have a back plate."

"I'll keep an eye out."

"Thanks. My contact information." He handed him a Blackwell business card.

Barnes pulled ahead and Mercedes stared out the window, watching a motorist get out of her car with a questioning look on her face.

Everyone was suspect. Even the innocent.

"What do you make of it?" he asked.

She was shocked that he wanted her opinion. "Rules out accidental drowning."

"You think so?" he eyed her.

She realized his rimless glasses acted as a shield, a barrier to keep anyone from seeing too deep into his thoughts.

"What do you think?" she shot back.

"It's quite a coincidence that two children from the same family have gone missing."

She squared off at him. "Why would a kidnapper hold Lucas for three days without a ransom demand? And why pick the same week to abduct the sister when you know that the family will be surrounded by cops?"

"Arrogance? You have to accept it."

"Maybe," she whispered. The very word she'd used to describe Jeremy. Yet she was starting to reconsider.

She'd enjoyed their interaction and brainstorming

about the case. It was as if they're opposite natures created a new kind of energy, a balanced energy.

They pulled up to the Weddles' driveway. The house sitting on the other side of the iron gates was big enough for five families.

"Yes?" a voice said through the intercom.

"Agents Barnes and Ramos from the Blackwell Group."

The gate squeaked open. A few unmarked and Mountain View police cars lined up to the house. Two uniforms stood on the front landing, smoking cigarettes. Jeremy pulled behind a dark sedan and they got out.

"Follow my lead," he said to her.

She didn't take offense this time.

They approached the two men. "Good afternoon. I'm Jeremy Barnes, this is Mercedes Ramos. The Weddles have hired us to investigate their son's disappearance," Barnes said. "I understand the daughter's gone missing?"

"The call came in a half hour ago," the taller of the two men said. "The chief is inside trying to calm down the grandmother. She's the one who called it in."

"What's the status of the search?" Barnes asked.

"They're combing the property and have started a neighborhood search. We're trying to figure out how the perp got into the house. I mean look at the security." He motioned toward the gates.

"Who was on the premises besides the grandmother?" Mercedes asked.

"The gardener, he's in the dining room being questioned. Housekeeper, she's already been questioned. She's helping keep the grandmother calm."

"Thanks," Barnes said and went into the mansion.

The foyer was as large as Mercedes's house growing up. What did one family need with so much space? She struggled to get her objectivity back.

Voices drifted into the entryway from where she guessed was the living room.

"Grandmother first?"

"I'd like to look around. Can you interview her?" He paused and looked at her. "But be gentle."

"Aren't I always?" she shot back, half teasing. She knew her style wasn't warm and fuzzy. That was Mercedes. She had to act tough in a man's world.

They parted and Jeremy headed upstairs. It was a large home, a little larger than his family house. He always wondered why they needed such a big house since he was an only child. Later, as a teenager, he figured out it had been a status symbol, a way to show the rest of the world how important the Barnes family was. Which made matters worse when they'd sold it during the divorce. He and Mum ended up in a modest flat and his father moved into a handsome home in Primrose Hill.

Not that Jeremy had ever seen it. His father only

showed interest in his son when Jeremy said he planned to study law. Then Edward made time to offer advice about which area of study would earn the best wage.

A hefty income is the key to happiness.

Strange thing, his father never seemed happy. He seemed dissatisfied and critical of the world. Especially of his son.

Jeremy walked into what he assumed was Lucas's room. Stars covered the dark blue ceiling. Envy coursed through him that the boy's parents let him deface his room with stars, posters and mobiles. They obviously understood Lucas's creative brilliance and were supportive. Lucky boy.

He went to the boy's desk and tapped the computer keyboard. The screen lit up with instant message notifications. Multiple windows flashed across the sky blue background; messages inviting Lucas to converse. For a shy boy, he had plenty of online friends. Jeremy jotted down some of the instant message names for Eddie, in case they were lost when he unplugged the machine.

The boy's room was in impeccable shape, which meant he was the organized type. Actually, it reminded Jeremy of his own room.

Jeremy had spent much of his childhood there, the only place he'd felt truly comfortable. Being smart made you different—a freak.

He wondered if Lucas felt the same way. At ten,

there was nothing worse than thinking you were different. Or unloved.

It was obvious Lucas's parents loved him very much and they showed it by letting him design his room to best reflect his interests.

Jeremy remembered wanting to hide from the cruelties and disappointments of his life. Of course, at the time he didn't understand those feelings. He drifted off into fantasyland, creating a secret castle in his closet where he'd save princesses from dragons and hold summit meetings with his imaginary team of Master Fighters.

Smiling, he opened the closet door. It was fantastic, large enough to be a small bedroom. Clothes lined one wall and a playhouse sat against the other side. He crouched down and opened the playhouse door.

And there, curled up in a ball, thumb in her mouth, lay a little girl—Lucas's sister, Natalia, no doubt.

Her eyes popped open and she whimpered.

He eased out of the house and sat, cross-legged on the floor. "Don't be scared. I'm Jeremy. I'm here to help find Lucas."

She blinked, a tear trickling down her cheek.

"You miss your brother, don't you?"

She nodded, not taking her thumb out of her mouth.

"Why are you hiding in here?"

She blinked.

"Is this Lucas's special place?"

She nodded. "I wanted to find him."

"But he wasn't here?"

She shook her head.

"Everyone's looking for you."

"I want Lucas."

"I know, love. We all want to find him."

"Lucas is a big boy," she said.

"We'll find him. But first I need to tell everyone I found you. Can you come out?"

She blinked.

"Please? I need your help finding your brother."

She unfolded her body and crawled out of the house, right into Jeremy's lap.

"That's a good girl," he said, trying to act like he knew what to do with thirty pounds of little girl. She wrapped her arms around his neck and he closed his eyes, absorbing her complete trust.

"Shall we find your grandmother?"

"Okay."

While holding her against him, he awkwardly got up.

Mercedes stood in the doorway. "What's this?"

Natalia whimpered and buried her face against Jeremy's shoulder.

"Lucas's little sister went looking for him and fell asleep in the closet."

"I'll let them know she's been found."

"Thanks. Ask the grandmother to come up here, alone, will you? Natalia's upset enough as it is."

"Sure." She winked. "You're a natural."

Bloody hell he was. She was good at taunting him, driving home his shortcomings. He knew he didn't have the parent gene. Although, if he were to become a father, he'd work a hell of a lot harder at it than Edward and Elizabeth Barnes.

Now, what was he thinking? Being a parent was not in Jeremy's future. He knew nothing about raising a confident child. Any child of Jeremy's would undoubtedly think him cross all the time because he kept such a tight rein on his feelings and emotions.

It had been the best coping mechanism for the emotional beatings he'd taken as a child. The best coping mechanism for life.

"Natalia, how's your brother been lately? Happy or sad?"

"Sad," she whispered into his ear.

His chest tightened at the feel of her sweet breath against his skin.

"Why do you say that?"

"I break his things and Daddy doesn't play with him anymore." She leaned back and looked at Jeremy. "Lucas is a big boy."

"My God, Natalia!" The grandmother raced into the room, her arms outstretched.

Natalia clung tighter to Jeremy's neck.

"I think your grandmother needs a hug," he encouraged.

"I want Lucas." Her voice muffled against his shoulder.

He turned and said into her ear, "If I'm to find him I need you to go to your grandmother, okay, love?"

She nodded, leaned back and looked into his eyes. For a second it seemed like she could read his thoughts. God, he hoped not. She'd know how utterly incompetent he really felt about comforting her.

"You talk funny," she said.

He smiled and passed her to the grandmother.

"Natalia, you scared me!" Grandmother said. "Don't ever do that again. Don't you know everyone was looking for you?"

Don't make her feel ashamed, Jeremy thought. She missed her brother.

"They'll understand," he said.

"Where did you find her?"

"In the playhouse in Lucas's closet."

The grandmother looked into Natalia's eyes. "Didn't you hear me calling you?"

"She fell asleep," Jeremy offered, wishing she'd say the right thing.

And what was that, exactly?

"I want Lucas," the little girl whimpered.

"I know, sshhh, I know," the grandmother consoled, patting the child's back.

"We're going to borrow Lucas's computer and be on our way," Jeremy said.

The elderly woman nodded and started out of the

room. “I was so scared,” she said to the little girl. “I love you so much, Natalia.”

There it was—the words he’d been waiting for.

Her head popped up from her grandmother’s shoulder and Natalia smiled. “Bye, Jeremy.”

“Bye,” was all he could say. So innocent, so trusting. And safe. Thank God.

“Someone’s got a crush on you,” Mercedes teased.

“Surprises you, does it?” He refocused on getting the computer.

“Not at all,” she said, casually.

Was she flirting with him?

“How did you know?” She grabbed the keyboard.

“Know what?”

“That she’d be hiding in the closet?”

“I didn’t,” he said.

“Then what made you look in there?”

He unplugged the power cord and wrapped it around the CPU. “I was trying to get a sense of Lucas’s state of mind when he sat in this room.”

“And that led you into a dark closet?”

“Didn’t you ever imagine things when you were a kid? Play pretend games?”

“Sure, but I didn’t peg you for the *imaginary friend* type.”

The imaginary ones were the best kind, he thought, remembering the cruel classmates that taunted him. If it wasn’t for being teacher’s pet, then it was his looks—tall, skinny, with glasses. A perfect target.

He remembered asking for karate classes for his thirteenth birthday, but Mum said she couldn't risk the hospital bills if he got hurt. He suffered two more years of cruel jokes and bullying. Then he got a paper delivery job and used his wages to take karate, without Mum's knowledge. It gave him strength; it gave him confidence.

Yet somewhere, deep down, he was still fighting the scrawny image of himself every time he looked in the mirror.

He headed down the stairs, CPU in hand. He glanced at a photograph of Lucas on the wall, wearing a button-down shirt, tie and forced grin. Jeremy wondered if part of the motivation behind homeschooling him was to protect him.

It sounded like the father had been a prodigy, making his first million by age thirty. He probably remembered what it was like—the teasing, the practical tricks. Is that why they kept the boy home? To shelter him?

"Keys are in my pocket," he said.

"I'll hold the computer. I don't want you accusing me of sexual harassment." She grabbed the CPU from his arms.

Was she uncomfortable at the thought of touching him?

Just as well. When she'd touched his shoulder

before an odd sensation had shot down his arm. He'd probably just gone too long without a decent female connection.

Listen to yourself. You sound so bloody clinical.

She put the computer in the trunk and he closed it. He didn't have much contact with women, other than the rare female agent, a handful of sexual encounters and his new friendship with Cassie.

It was strange how Max had initially seemed jealous when Cassie touched Jeremy. But Jeremy knew it was a touch of friendship, not attraction. She seemed more like a little sister than a seductive woman.

God, man, if you can't be attracted to that girl, there must be something seriously wrong with you.

He always suspected as much. Why else would Nancy have left him without so much as a goodbye note, or a postcard from whatever exotic country she'd run off to?

Had she decided there could be no real future between them because of the age difference? She'd mentioned wanting to have children, which was natural since she was in her twenties, but the thought terrified him. And not because he was only eighteen and she was twenty-five. He feared fatherhood because he hadn't a clue how a good father behaved.

"You have directions to the Lynk place?" Mercedes asked.

"In the folder." He nodded to the seat between them and started the car.

"What's up?" She opened the folder, but was staring at Jeremy.

"Excuse me?"

"You're out there, in la-la land."

"Probably still recovering from the flu."

"No, something else is bothering you. Is it the little girl?"

God, could she see it? How the few minutes holding Natalia opened up all his childhood wounds?

"What's bothering me is we still don't have a feeling for the boy's state of mind when he disappeared." He steered down the driveway.

"What are you looking for?" she asked.

Besides peace?

"A direction, for one."

"Take this back to the highway and turn left."

"I didn't mean that kind of direction."

She cocked her head to one side.

"It's like we're all flailing about, trying to find the boy, but we're ignoring the life boat in front of us."

"Meaning?"

"Put yourself in his place. How was he feeling that day? What was he thinking?"

"He was probably happy to be at the ocean with the other kids."

"Was he?"

"What do you mean?"

"I'm guessing that being a shy boy, his social skills weren't top caliber."

"Which could make him awkward around a group of thirty kids. You think he might have been overwhelmed?"

"Possibly."

"Then why would he wander off from the group?"

"Maybe Shayne Lynk can give us some insight into that question," he said.

She directed him to turn onto a heavily wooded street. They found the house, a modest Tudor, tucked away on an acre of land.

"You want to conduct this interview?" he asked.

"No, thanks. You're the natural with kids."

He clenched his jaw and headed for the house. She couldn't be more wrong. Still, he hoped the boy could give Jeremy a feel for what was going on in Lucas's life.

They were greeted by the grandfather. "David said to expect you. I'm Burt, Shayne's grandfather. Shayne is out back with a friend."

"Thanks."

"This is Lilianna, my wife," Burt said.

"Something to drink?" the older woman offered as they passed through the kitchen.

"No thank you," Jeremy said.

"Actually, I'd love a glass of water." Mercedes nodded at Jeremy to go outside.

He got the message. She'd ask the grandparents

some questions and let Jeremy do the interview alone. Probably a good idea not to gang up on the boy.

It was strange how Jeremy could read her mind, how in sync they had become after only hours of working together.

The grandfather opened the slider to the backyard. "Shayne?"

"Yeah, Gramps?"

"An investigator is here to talk to you about Lucas."

A boy with bright blond hair and a blue striped shirt sprung out of the bushes, a taller boy beside him.

"What were you doing back there?" the grandfather asked.

"Nothing." Shayne glanced at his mud-covered shoes.

"Sit down and speak with this man."

Jeremy sat at the table, Shayne and his friend across from him.

"They haven't found him yet, huh?" the other boy said.

He seemed like the bossy type, Jeremy thought.

"Not yet."

"He's dead," Bossy Boy stated.

"Shut up," Shayne protested.

The grandfather disappeared in the bushes where the boys had been playing.

"What's your name?" he asked the friend.

"Brad Reynolds. Hey, you're from England. Where? London, like the Beatles?"

"The Beatles were from Liverpool," Jeremy corrected.

Brad narrowed his eyes.

"Shayne Michael Lynk! What is this?" The grandfather marched across the lawn with a pack of cigrettes in his hand.

Shayne's cheeks flushed. Brad leaned back in his chair, a smirk spreading across his face.

"Smoking? You're sneaking away and smoking cigarettes?" He turned to Brad. "It's time you go home."

The friend pushed away from the table and stormed off.

"We'll talk about this later," the grandfather said. "After you finish with the detective." He went into the house. "Can you believe this? He's smoking cigarettes in the bushes," he said to his wife as he shut the sliding glass door.

Shayne's eyes welled up with tears.

You're a baby. Be a man! A voice taunted Jeremy. His mother's voice.

"Not very smart, the whole cigarette thing," Jeremy said. "You know why?"

Shayne sniffled and shook his head.

"First off, it's against the law. You're not eighteen yet, are you?"

He shook his head.

"Secondly, it's one of those terrible habits that is hard to break. And you'll want to break it because it can kill you."

"I know."

Jeremy cocked his head to the side. "You know? Then why did you smoke?"

"Because Brad said smoking is what men do and I wasn't a man if I didn't smoke."

"I'm a man and I don't smoke."

The boy shrugged.

"Trust me, smoking is stupid."

He glanced up at Jeremy. "That's what Lucas said."

"Lucas is a smart boy."

"Brad called him a baby."

"He did? Why?"

"He said Lucas couldn't do anything without his parents. He needed them for school, for friends, everything."

"Do *you* believe that?"

He shrugged.

"What else did Brad say?"

"That Lucas couldn't survive without his parents, that his mom and dad spoil him and that he doesn't know what it's like to be a real kid."

"A real kid? What an odd expression. What does that mean?"

"Lucas doesn't go to school." He counted on his

fingers. "He has a full-time maid, he's driven everywhere, they even go to Hawaii for vacation."

"And Brad doesn't go to Hawaii?"

"Nope. Went to Mount St. Helens once, but that's only a couple of hours from here."

"Do you like this boy? Brad?" Jeremy asked.

"I guess."

"Did Lucas like him?"

"Not so much."

"He sounds like a bully."

The boy's gaze shot up to connect with Jeremy's. "He is kind of mean sometimes."

"To Lucas?"

He nodded.

"What about Lucas's other friends?" Jeremy prompted.

"He didn't really have any live ones."

"I'm sorry?"

"He had lots of friends online. We all do."

Jeremy's mobile vibrated against his breast pocket. "Excuse me," he said to the boy, stood and walked to the edge of the wooden deck. "Barnes."

"You'd better get back here, mate," Max said. "They got a ransom note."

Chapter Six

Her partner was unusually quiet on the drive back to the Command Center. Mercedes studied his profile wondering what was going on in that head of his.

Was it something the Lynk boy said or had she upset him somehow? She hated not being able to read this man.

Yet, back at the Weddle home she could read the feelings in his eyes when he held the little girl, feelings of regret and sadness. Why? He was a young man in his thirties with plenty of time to marry and have children.

"Why so quiet?" she said, uncomfortable with the silence.

"I have nothing to say."

"You're upset with me?"

He glanced at her, his blue eyes questioning. "Why would you think that?"

"I don't know what to think. You play your cards pretty close."

He cracked a smile. "You'll know when I'm cross with you."

"Thanks for the warning." She crossed her arms over her chest. "This news about the ransom is good. Now we have something to work with."

"I suppose."

More silence. She couldn't stand it. It reminded her of her older cousin, Rosita, who would ignore Mercedes because she'd borrowed earrings without asking. The silence was worse than a shouting match.

The man sitting next to her was not quiet because he was angry with Mercedes, however. Something else bothered him and she hadn't a clue what.

When she'd caught him holding the little girl, Mercedes's heart warmed. It seemed like such a sweet and tender gesture from someone she thought cold as the iceberg that destroyed the *Titanic*. She never thought she'd see that kind of compassion from this controlled man.

His behavior with the little girl was inconsistent with his job and his personality. Then again, maybe he was married with children and she assumed wrongly from the start.

"How many children do you have?" she asked.

"I'm not married."

"Oh, I thought, because of the way you were with the little girl that you had experience."

"No experience. You?"

"No kids, but I take my nieces for overnights a few times a year."

"How old are they?"

"Five, seven and nine."

"You're brave."

"My sister is the brave one. Three kids within five years of each other. My brother, Enrique has three, as well. Thank goodness. The pressure's off me."

"Even with all those grandchildren, your parents want more from you?"

"Absolutely. What about you?"

He focused out the front window. "I don't need to provide them with grandchildren."

"You're an only child and your parents aren't on your back for grandchildren?"

"Elizabeth would be horrified to be called grandmother." He smiled.

Mercedes realized that on the rare occasion he shot her that smile, his whole affect changed from cold and aloof, to warm and mischevious. He was quite handsome, in a classic sort of way.

"What?" he said.

"Huh?"

"You're eyeing me strangely."

"Sorry. I can't imagine being an only child."

Good recovery.

"It must have been wonderful," she said. "No one fighting over the last brownie, no one stealing your clothes, no one beating up on you."

His smiled faded.

"So, what insight does my only child partner have about our missing boy?" she asked, wanting to distract him, to change that sad expression on his face.

"I think he felt different and very alone."

Her partner's expression didn't change. And she wondered if he was talking about the lost boy, or about himself. Her heart went out to Jeremy.

Watch yourself, Mercedes.

Pulling into town, they found a parking spot, grabbed the computer and headed for the office.

"Let's hope Eddie finds a lead on who could have taken Lucas," Jeremy said. "The Lynk boy said Lucas had quite a few online friends."

"When are these kids going to learn?" She opened the door for him.

"They're kids. They don't think they're in danger by chatting it up online."

He slid the computer to Eddie's desk.

"Gifts, thank you!" Eddie said.

"The boy's computer," Jeremy explained. "He had a lot of Internet friends, so you might want to check that activity first."

"Sure, boss. Max and Cassie are with the Weddles. Spinelli and Finn are trying to bust their way into the official command post for the latest scoop."

"Wouldn't they be better off charming their way in?" Mercedes said.

"They don't have natural charisma," he said smiling. "Like me."

Jeremy was getting tired of every male on the team flirting with his partner.

"You've got charisma with a computer, you mean," Jeremy clarified.

"I don't know, I've been told I've got people charisma." He winked at Mercedes.

She smiled back at him.

"Whenever you two are done, we'll get back to work."

She stuck out her tongue.

"Mature," Jeremy said.

Eddie laughed, a young, robust sound that made Jeremy jealous.

Jeremy went to his desk, eyeing a brown box.

"Max wants you to meet them at the lodge," Eddie offered. "Local cops and FBI are in charge, but the Weddles requested members of Blackwell be allowed to observe."

"Observe, my ass," Mercedes muttered.

"Oh, yeah," Eddie said to Jeremy. "That box was delivered about an hour ago. If it's candy I want some."

"I haven't a clue what it is," Jeremy whispered.

Mercedes glanced at her mobile. "My little sister's calling. I'll wait for you outside."

He refocused on the box. There were no stamps on it, which meant it hadn't come through the post, and on the top was a label with rather messy handwriting. It was addressed to Inspector Jeremy Barnes.

He cut along the taped edges and opened the flaps. A typed note lay on top of a mound of white foam packaging.

Abandoned by his own father.
How does it feel?

The blood rushed to his head and he sat down, the note pinched between his fingers.

What on earth was this about? Another threat? Or did this refer to the Weddle case?

He glanced up to see if Eddie was watching. Luckily, the bloke was intent on breaking into the Weddle boy's computer.

Jeremy tipped the box to empty the peanuts into the trash bin. He spotted something dark among the packaging and grabbed it. It snapped at his finger.

"Bloody hell!" he swore, dropping the box. Pinching the life out of his fingers was a mousetrap. He pried the metal off his fingers and shook them.

"You okay, sir?" Eddie started to get up.

He shoved the note into his inside jacket pocket. "Fine."

"What's up?" Mercedes asked, coming into the room. She glanced at his swelling fingers. "What happened?"

"Went for my pen and got my fingers stuck in a mousetrap."

She shook her head. "A mousetrap?"

"It was a practical joke, a private joke."

"Doesn't seem very funny to me."

"Let's go." He made for the door. He could use an aspirin to dull the pain, but he didn't want to look weak to his partner.

"Barnes?" she said.

He turned and she tossed a bottle of something at him. Pain reliever.

"Don't be macho." She went to the water cooler, filled a cup and brought it to him. "I've lived with macho my whole life and I'm bored with it."

"I'm fine," he said.

"I know, but it hurts me to look at your fingers so take the pills, okay?"

She opened the bottle and handed him two pills. He put them into his mouth and drank the water.

"Dios mio." Gripping his wrist, she laid his injured fingers in her open palm to scrutinize them more carefully. "We need to get you some ice."

Something about her touch unnerved him, a nurturing touch that warmed his skin. Even Nancy's touch was more sexual than nurturing, more ravenous than compassionate.

He snatched his hand back. "Don't. We need to go."

"But you need ice."

He walked out on her protest, needing distance. Sure, his fingers throbbed, but that pain wasn't nearly as bad as the ache filling his chest, knowing only now what he'd been missing in his life.

And he'd felt it from a woman who didn't even like him.

He started for Eagle Lodge, hoping she'd give him space. Embarrassed by his reaction to her touch, he realized he acted like a thirteen-year-old boy running from an unexpected kiss.

Blast, now he was thinking about kissing her?

No, that could never happen. Even if she weren't a work associate, he'd never get involved with a woman like Mercedes, a passionate woman who could easily get through his defenses. Look what a mere touch had done to him. She was the type of woman who could get to his core. And that scared the hell out of him.

Trying to refocus on the case, he picked up his stride and crossed the street.

"Watch out!" Mercedes cried.

He hesitated just as a blue car raced around the corner. Jeremy jumped out of the way and landed against the curb.

"Hey! Hey!" Mercedes cried after the motorist. She kneeled beside him. "Are you okay?"

"Fine." He got to his feet, favoring his left leg. He jammed his knee in the fall. He studied her worried eyes. "I really am fine."

"Are you okay, sir?" a middle-aged man asked, jogging toward them.

"Yes, thank you."

"Lucky thing your wife called out that warning," he said.

Jeremy glanced at Mercedes whose brows knitted together in concern.

"What's the matter with you?" she demanded. "Didn't you see him speeding around the corner?"

"No, I did not." He'd been distracted, thinking about her. Not good.

"Do you want me to hang around for the police report?" the witness offered. "I got a partial plate number."

Jeremy and Mercedes looked at him.

"I watch *CSI,*" he explained.

"I'm not involving the police," Jeremy said. "But we'd appreciate the plate number. We're with a private detective agency so we can look into it ourselves."

"Sure, it started with five-four-three and then I think an *H*."

"Thanks," Jeremy said, shaking the man's hand.

"Is he okay?" a woman said, running out of a gift shop on the corner.

Jeremy looked at Mercedes. "Let's be off before I make local headlines."

"Thanks again," Mercedes said to the middle-aged man. She held on to Jeremy's arm as they walked toward the lodge.

"I said I'm fine." He eyed her hand that gently gripped his upper arm.

"Good, I'm glad. I'm not. I'm still shaken up because I saw him hit you."

"He didn't hit me." He continued walking. "Thanks to your warning."

"He didn't even brake. Jerk."

"Did you get a good look at him?"

"No, but it almost seemed like he meant to hit you." She shook her head. "I'll call in the plate to Eddie. Maybe he can track down the driver." She pulled out her phone, but didn't let go of his arm.

"Probably a teenager," he said.

"Who needs his license revoked," she added. She called Eddie and gave him the information. "He's on it." She flipped her mobile closed and eyed him. "I'm starting to wonder if you're a bad luck partner. First the truck, now this. I'd better watch myself around you."

She didn't know how close she was to the truth. That's it. He wouldn't put her in danger any longer.

"You're right, you deserve a partner with better luck," he said. "How about Bobby Finn? He's Irish."

She stopped and stared him down. "Hey, you get me reassigned and who's going to look after you? No, you need a tough woman blessed with good luck to take care of you."

"That's you, is it?" He opened the door to the lodge and she broke contact.

"Sure, sure. You know I'm tough. As for my luck, well, I won the lottery last year."

He shot her a look of disbelief.

"Twelve bucks." She nodded. Very proud of herself.

Jeremy puzzled over her new, friendly nature. It was as if she were trying to divert his attention away from what had just happened. She cared enough to bother?

They arrived at the Weddles' hotel room and found it buzzing with police, FBI and family. Jeremy spotted Max in the corner with Cassie and Mrs. Weddle.

Mrs. Weddle nodded at Jeremy and Mercedes, then went into her husband's waiting arms. The man closed his eyes as he hugged his wife. He must feel completely helpless.

"The drop is scheduled for tomorrow at five in the evening," Max said. "Mr. Weddle will take a backpack with one hundred thousand dollars to a wine shop on Main Street and leave it in the loo."

"Tomorrow? Why wait until tomorrow?" Mercedes asked.

"It's the opening of the Coastal Wine Festival," Max said. "There will be thousands of people filling the streets, muddling up the investigation."

"Why only one hundred thousand?" Jeremy asked.

"Wondering that myself, mate. With all the millions Mr. Weddle has to part with, why ask for only a fraction?"

"Not a sophisticated kidnapper, guv," Jeremy said.

"No indeed."

Max eyed an FBI agent as he coached Mr. Weddle on his role as drop-off man.

"Max," Jeremy said, pulling him aside. "I need to speak with you about Mercedes."

"Is she that difficult to work with?"

Jeremy didn't want to get her sacked. He just wanted to keep her safe which meant as far away from him as possible.

"It's not that, guv. I'm concerned about—"

"Everyone out!" Mr. Weddle's outburst interrupted their discussion. "I can't think with all these people around."

"And I thought I had a temper," Mercedes muttered.

"That's mild compared to my reaction if my son had been taken," Jeremy said.

Mercedes, Cassie and Max stared at him as if they couldn't imagine him losing control.

"What?" he asked.

The lead FBI agent motioned for his team to vacate the room. "That means you, too," he ordered Max.

"Actually, you're not paying for my services. He is." Max motioned toward Mr. Weddle.

"They stay," Weddle said.

Max shrugged. The FBI bloke's head looked like it was about to explode. He finished gathering his people and started out the door, then turned to Mr. Weddle. "I'm leaving Agent Watts. You won't even know he's here. There will be two agents posted outside the door."

Weddle waved him off. They left and Mr. Weddle motioned for the Blackwell members to sit down.

Jeremy remained standing by the window. Feeling distanced from the group helped him analyze the situation with a clear head.

Right, like his head was clear after the threatening notes, the mousetrap and wild motorist? He noticed Mercedes was studying him from across the room. She deserved to know the truth, the whole team did.

Which was what exactly? That he'd attracted a stalker? Blast, he needed to get with Eddie, look into old case files, do something to end this. Later, after they found the little boy. Finding Lucas was the priority.

"How did you receive the ransom request?" Max asked Mr. Weddle.

"E-mail."

"Would you mind if our computer expert popped in to have a look? He's exceptional with these things."

"Sure." Mr. Weddle leaned back into the sofa and his wife leaned against his chest.

"We'd like a print out, as well, for our entire team," Max said.

Weddle nodded.

"The next twenty-four hours are going to be horrible and I'm sorry," Max continued. "But the good news is, if you do what the kidnapper asks he has no reason to harm Lucas."

"I don't like the FBI's plan," Mr. Weddle said, eyeing FBI Agent Watts, who sat in the corner. "They want to have someone waiting in the wine shop, someone who can tail the kidnapper after he picks up the money."

"It's insurance, to make sure they find Lucas," Max explained.

"It could mess the whole thing up."

"Mr. Weddle," Jeremy said. "To get a jump on things, it would help us to know if you can think of anyone, enemies, perhaps, who would orchestrate a kidnapping."

"Enemies? Try software companies I put out of business or the first company I bought out, Nigitcorp, or how about the old friends who suddenly called to chat after they found out I'd become a millionaire, or hell, I don't know."

"Shhh," his wife consoled, then looked at Jeremy. The pain in her eyes tore at his heart. "We really don't know who would do this."

"Anyone who's come looking for money lately?" Max said. "You have a foundation designed for small businesses looking to get a start?"

"Yes."

"And what's your role?"

"I'm chairman of the board. I make the final decision. Contact Roxanne Drecker at the foundation office. She can give you a list of who we've rejected."

"I'd like to leave my agents here for the night," Max said. "Keep a watch on things."

"If you think it's a good idea."

"I do." Max stood and shook the man's hand. "Barnes and Ramos, I'll leave you in charge. Barnes, we'll finish our discussion tomorrow. Mercedes, I need a moment."

"Yes, sir." She followed Max into the hallway.

Now what was that about, Jeremy wondered.

He felt someone touch his arm. He glanced into Mrs. Weddle's eyes.

"This is good, right?" she queried.

"Yes, very good." He smiled.

Her husband paced the living area.

"Can I get you anything?" Jeremy asked Mr. Weddle.

"You mean besides my son? Dammit." Weddle went out onto the balcony.

His wife followed, closing the sliding door behind her. She rubbed his back and leaned into him. With arms spread across the balcony rail, Doug Weddle hung his head. His body shook, probably with tears of frustration.

Mercedes came back into the room, holding out her mobile. "You've got a call. If I'm going to play secretary I need a raise." She winked.

He took the phone. "Hello?"

"Bastard," a computerized voice said.

"Excuse me?"

"You owe me, Barnes. Carver's Cove—2 a.m. Come alone."

Chapter Seven

It was the only way to figure out what the hell was going on, Jeremy thought as he snuck across the room. He glanced over his shoulder. Mercedes was sound asleep in a chair, Eddie was still working on Mr. Weddle's computer, the FBI agent was watching the telly without the sound.

"I've got to run out," Jeremy whispered. "Need some air."

Eddie didn't respond.

Jeremy touched his shoulder and Eddie looked up. "Huh?"

"I can't sleep. I'm going to get some air."

"Sure, okay." He snapped his attention back to the computer screen.

Jeremy closed the door softly, not wanting to wake Mercedes. She needed her sleep. And he needed to take care of this alone.

You owe me, Barnes.

The computerized voice haunted him. What

haunted him even more was that the call came in on Mercedes's mobile, not Jeremy's. Jeremy hadn't meant to put her at risk; he'd tried to tell Max he couldn't be paired with her, for her own good.

No, that wasn't his only motivation. She was starting to sense things about him, things better left alone—like his secret ache to feel a child's love.

Walking down Main Street, Jeremy headed for the beach. He'd done his research earlier, when he'd convinced Mercedes to pick up dinner for them. That hadn't been easy. He could see that she didn't want to be perceived as a low-level assistant, but when he'd made up an excuse about being sore from the car incident, she willingly volunteered.

He'd played upon her nurturing instinct and it had worked. Sneaking a few minutes on Eddie's computer, Jeremy had discovered that Carver's Cove was only blocks from the lodge, off the main beach.

He flipped up his collar against the chill. A lot like back home, he admitted, blowing into his hands. Fall could be a dark and unforgiving season, especially to people like the Weddles, who ached for their kidnapped son.

Kidnapped by whom?

The big question topping the list and Jeremy couldn't focus with his personal issue distracting him.

Someone was out to get him.

And he hadn't a clue why.

He wracked his brain for potential enemies, former criminals he'd put away for life. None stood out more than another and he'd never grown intimate enough with a woman to warrant this kind of anger.

Sure, he'd been intimate with Nancy, but she had no right to hold a grudge. She'd been the one who'd left him. He'd tried to find her, pressed her roommate and friends, but no one knew where she'd gone. They just knew she was safe…and happy.

Without Jeremy.

He reached Third Street and turned left, heading for the ocean. Not sure what tonight would bring, he'd carried his service revolver for protection. He fingered the cool steel clipped to his belt. Maybe he should have notified Templeton of his troubles.

No, Jeremy would resolve this on his own.

Stepping onto the unstable sand, Jeremy wished he'd changed into his trainers. It would have made this hike to the cove a bit easier.

He spotted a few bonfires on the beach, teenagers, no doubt, still partying. He wished they'd move on. He didn't want to put innocents in harm's way.

Like Mercedes. She was an innocent in this confusing mess and he didn't want to see her hurt. But it was more than that. She intrigued him, challenged his calm nature like no other woman—or man—ever had. Even Templeton couldn't set Jeremy's temper off like his sexy partner.

Bugger, she *was* sexy as hell. Good thing he wasn't in the market for romance.

No. He was only capable of having casual affairs. He couldn't risk anything deeper, couldn't risk anyone finding out that he was missing something inside. Why else would Nancy have abandoned him?

The sound of a child whimpering made him stop short. He glanced toward the ocean, then back toward the cove, trying to get an idea of where it was coming from but it was nearly impossible to pinpoint the source.

"Hello?" he called.

More whimpering echoed from the cove.

He picked up his pace, ignoring the soreness lingering in his knee from the car accident.

"Help me," a voice cried.

He raced toward the sound, the tide rushing onto the sand, slowing his feet, feeling like he was running in mud, mud that seemed to weigh down his shoes.

"I'm coming!" he called out, racing between two huge rocks toward the ocean.

But his foot caught on something and he fell flat to the sand, the wind knocked from his lungs.

He struggled to catch his breath and started to push up with his hands. Someone jumped on top of him, ripped off his glasses and shoved his cheek into the sand.

"Don't move, you wanker," a voice said.

A voice with a British accent.

"What the bloody hell is this about?" Jeremy demanded, struggling to get his advantage back.

"It's about vengeance, mate. Eighteen years' worth."

A cord wrapped around Jeremy's neck and pinched his windpipe. Slipping his fingers between the rope and his skin, he struggled to breathe.

"I had a surprise waiting, but you ran off the wrong way," his attacker said. "Idiot inspector."

"Can't we talk about this like civilized men?"

"That would be assuming I'm civilized." He leaned closer. "I'm not."

He yanked on the cord and Jeremy yanked back, refusing to be bested by this twit.

"Barnes!" Mercedes's voice called from a distance.

"Bugger," the attacker said. "Next time you won't be saved by a woman." He ripped the cord from Jeremy's throat, burning his skin.

Jeremy coughed and felt for his glasses, as the blurred form of his assailant disappeared toward the larger of the two rocks.

"Barnes, what the hell?" Mercedes fell to her knees beside him.

"Forget about me, go get him." She started to get up. "No, don't." He grabbed her wrist. He didn't want her going off alone, putting herself in danger because of him. "My glasses, do you see them?"

"Here." She handed them to him.

He stood, blew on his specs and started after his attacker.

"You want to tell me what the hell is going on?" she demanded.

"I don't know."

"You don't know?" she said, jogging beside him. "You don't know who called earlier, or why a car would almost hit you on the street or why a truck would nearly run us off the road?"

She grabbed his arm to get his attention. He glanced at her, but kept a quick pace.

"What are we dealing with here?" she demanded.

"Vengeance."

"Excuse me?"

"That's what he's calling it."

"You know him?" Her voice squeaked.

"No. Yes. I don't know."

"How long has this been going on?"

"I'm not sure. A day. Maybe longer."

"And you didn't say anything, but I get the lecture about being a team player?"

"I thought I could handle it alone."

"I can't believe this." She pointed down the beach. "Look, a campfire. Is that a man sitting there? What, is he waiting for us?"

"Do you have your firearm?"

"Yes."

He slipped his from his belt and they closed in on the campfire. Jeremy sneaked up behind him, motioning for her to stay behind cover. She narrowed her eyes and approached from the man's side.

Jeremy couldn't protect her if she walked into the man's line of fire.

Four feet away. Three. Two…

"Don't move." Jeremy pressed the barrel of his gun against the back of the man's head.

The man toppled over, a skull staring up at him from the sand.

He holstered his firearm.

"What kind of a sick joke is that?" she asked.

Then he noticed a name tag on the skeleton's coat. It read, *Jeremy Barnes.* He snapped it off and slipped it into his trouser pocket.

"Look at this. A tape recorder." She pressed a button with her knuckle and it played sounds of a child whimpering and calling out for help.

"Sick, sick." She snapped it off.

Jeremy glanced up the bluff to a few hotels, then back to the ocean. "Did you see which way he went? I thought he headed toward the water."

"I didn't notice. I was worried about you."

He glanced at her; her eyes blazed fire at him.

"What's your problem?" she said. "I'm your partner and you don't tell me some man is terrorizing you and wants to kill you?"

"We don't know that for sure."

She grabbed him by the shoulders. "Stop acting like this is another investigation. It's not, it's your life. Someone wants to kill you."

"If that were true, I'd be dead by now."

"How can you be so detached about this?"

He ignored her and glanced at the campfire. "We

should gather forensic evidence. I see a few cigarette butts." He knelt down and plucked one from the sand with his handkerchief.

The warmth of her hand set his cheek aflame. She turned his face to look into her eyes. "We're partners. You have to trust me."

"I can't." He had trusted deeply once and was betrayed.

She slipped her hand from his cheek and turned to walk away.

"Wait." He touched her shoulder.

She hesitated, planting her hands to her hips.

"It's not you. I haven't had a lot of luck trusting people."

She turned and stared him down, the wind blowing her long, dark hair across her face. "I'm not just people. I'm your partner."

A partner he wanted to kiss at this moment. Good God, he was losing his mind.

He snatched his hand back and shoved it into his pocket. "We'd better head back."

"I'll talk to Max in the morning," she said. "I can't work with a partner who doesn't take me into his confidence."

"I was trying to protect you."

"You were protecting yourself. You don't want people to know your secrets. Well, whatever secrets are after you, we can help. We're all a team."

"I'm sorry," he said. "I didn't want to involve you in this."

"Which is what?"

"I don't know."

She narrowed her eyes.

"On my honor, I truly don't know," he said.

He looked troubled, Mercedes thought, searching his eyes. Troubled and vulnerable. Jeremy Barnes was not the type to feel vulnerable.

You're fooling yourself. He doesn't need you.

The lost expression in his eyes spoke otherwise.

"Let's try and get some sleep." She reached out and squeezed his arm to comfort him. "It will be okay."

"I almost believe you."

"You should believe me." She started walking. "I never lie."

Holding on to his arm, they left the beach and headed down Main Street. It felt right to support him this way and not because Max had ordered her to watch over him. Her heart told her that this man needed a little compassion.

She remembered Curtis Sykes offering that same compassion when she thought her career ruined by the rumors swirling around her, rumors that she was having an affair with her partner, Will Crane.

It was all a lie, but it also had been easy to believe, especially since he'd put himself in harm's way for her. When on earth were men going to treat her as their equal and stop trying to protect her?

"You should have included me in your midnight walk," she said. "I'm a big girl. I can take care of myself."

As they approached the lodge, he slowed and said, "Why did you come looking for me tonight?"

She could tell him direct orders from Max sent her chasing after him.

But that would be a lie.

"It doesn't matter," he said, before she could answer. "Thank-you."

He leaned forward. God, he was going to kiss her. No, she didn't want to blow it again, ruin her chances at being taken seriously. She turned her face, but he must have been aiming for her cheek because his lips brushed against hers, so soft, warm and gentle.

Part of her welcomed the connection.

Not again. Don't ruin your career over a man.

She broke the kiss and stepped back. "I'm sorry, I mean you're welcome, I mean—"

"Shh." He placed his fingers to her lips.

She couldn't breathe.

"We'd both better get some sleep," he said.

"Right." She marched ahead of him.

She'd probably fall asleep and dream about seducing the sexy Brit with the wounded expression and hard body.

"Dios mio!" she muttered.

"Excuse me?" he said, coming up beside her as they waited for the elevator.

She smiled at him. "Nothing."

One thing was certain—she needed out of this partnership and she needed out yesterday.

WORK BEGAN IN THE COMMAND Center at nine the next morning. Everyone looked tired, Max thought, especially Barnes and Ramos. Were they up fighting all night?

Spinelli and Finn reported that they had come up empty. None of the locals saw anything outside of the ordinary the day Lucas Weddle went missing. Max moved on to Eddie.

"Nothing significant on the father's computer, no threatening e-mails in his incoming mail. Next, I'll check the spam history, then I'm going to work on the list of rejects from foundation requests."

"And what about the boy's computer?" Barnes asked.

"His recent Web searches were about campgrounds in the state of Oregon, how to start a fire, survival stuff mostly."

"Mercedes," Max said. "Check with the mother and see if his school curriculum included writing a report on survival in the wilderness."

"His mother mentioned something about the boy camping with the father," she said.

"He also joined a young scientists club, online," Eddie offered. "I found transcripts of chats. They host experts twice a month who talk about careers and scientific breakthroughs."

"Who attends these chats?" Max inquired.

"They're open to anyone who wants to join the club."

"Are you thinking pedophiles, sir?" Barnes asked.

"Possibly. Smart kids are easy targets. They tend to be book smart, but not people smart. Eddie, get screen names and see if you can match anything to a pedophile database."

"On it, sir."

Barnes seemed off in his own world. He'd come in this morning looking troubled. Maybe the Ramos match was more than he could handle.

"Right, well, let's try to find a lead before the money drop tonight. Barnes and I sense something odd about the ransom request and the fact the kidnapper is only asking for a hundred thousand dollars."

"I don't know, guv," Bobby said. "I could buy my ladies some fine presents with a hundred thousand."

"So that's how you get them to sleep with you?" Spinelli shot back.

Bobby flung his pen at his new partner.

"That's it, then." Max eyed Barnes. "Unless… Agent Barnes? Did you want to add something?"

"Actually, I do."

He walked to a more visible spot, very unlike him. Barnes liked to observe from the perimeter, take it all in and make assessments.

"Something happened last night," he started. "Actually, it's been happening for a few days. Odd things, really, but last night it became violent."

His gaze drifted to Agent Ramos, who was studying her notebook. She knew what he was about to say. Interesting. Had Barnes actually confided in his partner?

"It seems that someone is after me," Barnes said. "I don't know who. Now that I think about it, it may have started in Chicago. I remember waking up in the hospital to someone standing over my bed. More recently, things have been happening. I've received written threats and last night I was assaulted on the beach."

"And you didn't mention this sooner because?" Max pushed.

Barnes raised his chin a notch, but didn't answer.

"He thought he could handle it on his own," Mercedes offered.

"You knew about this?" Max said.

"No, she didn't," Jeremy interrupted.

Max found it interesting that he was trying to protect her.

"She didn't know until early this morning. She," Jeremy hesitated, "saved me on the beach."

"Saved you?" Max said, his temper flaring.

"I was lured to the beach and attacked from behind. He'd wrapped a cord around my throat when Agent Ramos showed up."

That's when Max noticed the redness around his neck.

"Good God, man, and you're just telling us this now?"

"I wasn't sure it was anything to be concerned about."

Agent Ramos shook her head.

"I was wrong." He glanced at the team, one by one. "I apologize for putting any of you in danger. I'll take my leave."

Barnes started for the door.

"Where in the bloody hell do you think you're going?" Max demanded.

Barnes turned to him.

"You've got a stalker and you've got some of the best detectives ready and willing to help you find him. I'd call you one lucky man."

"I don't want to distract us from the Weddle case and I didn't want to assume…"

"That we'd want to help you?" Max said. "Okay, team, who wants to help Agent Barnes find his tormentor?"

Mercedes was the first to raise her hand, followed by the rest of the group—Bobby, Joe, Eddie and Cassie.

"I don't want to put the Weddle case in jeopardy, guv."

"And I don't want to see your life in jeopardy, Barnes."

"Yes, sir."

"So, two cases at once, then. Should be no problem for a group of brilliant detectives," Max said. "What has your stalker said or done so far, in the way of clues?"

Just like that, Jeremy had a roomful of people who wanted to help him find his way out of this hell.

"Barnes?" Max said. "Don't look so surprised. We're a team."

Jeremy glanced at Mercedes and she smiled.

That smile encouraged him to spill it all to this group. Scary thing, friendship.

Is that what this was?

"It started with scribblings on a check at the restaurant," Jeremy started. "At first I thought it was for Mr. Weddle. It read *abandoned, lost* and *betrayed.* Next, I received a copy of an old newspaper clipping of a case I'd worked at Scotland Yard and I received a surprise gift, a mousetrap, with a note that read,

Abandoned by his own father. How does it feel?

Then, last night I got a call—"

"Wait," Mercedes interrupted. "The guy almost ran him down in the street yesterday and we nearly got run off the road on our way to Mountain View."

Max narrowed his eyes at Jeremy.

"We don't know the vehicle incidents are related," Jeremy said.

"Sure, we don't," she shot back.

"Who's telling this story?"

"Fine, fine." She put up her hand.

"Last night I got a phone call ordering me to meet at Carver's Cove. I heard a child whimpering, went to investigate and tripped on something. The assailant jumped me from behind. After Agent Ramos chased him off, we found a tape recorder with the child's voice and a skeleton."

"Wearing a name tag that read, *Jeremy Barnes,*" she added.

He shot her another warning glare.

"When he pinned me to the ground, he said it was about eighteen years of vengeance. I haven't a clue what he's talking about."

"Eddie," Max said, without missing a beat. "Search through records of Agent Barnes's arrests and convictions. See who was sentenced to an eighteen-year term."

"On it, sir. What about the pedophile search?"

"Ramos, call Agent Sykes and see if he can follow up on the pedophile angle."

"Yes, sir."

"Next, I don't want Barnes leaving this office," Max said.

Jeremy's heart sank. He'd be shackled to a desk when he needed to be out there, finding the boy.

"Unless he has a bodyguard," Max added.

"Ramos and Finn. You're assigned to Barnes. You'll be like the Three Musketeers."

"I'd rather not put other agents in danger," Jeremy said. Finn could take care of himself, but Jeremy did not want anything to happen to Mercedes because she was in the way.

Like last night? She'd taken care of herself and saved him, as well.

With his training he should have been able to save himself, but he'd been focused on a child's cries for help. Blast, he was starting to lose his perspective, letting the emotion of his case get to him.

"Agents are trained to defend themselves," Max said. "Where is the skeleton?"

"At Carver's Cove. I took the note." Barnes pulled out the note card with his name on it. "I also found a cigarette butt."

"Spinelli, you make any friends yet?" Max asked.

"As in forensic friends? Actually, I have."

"Good, you know what to do." Max motioned for Jeremy to give the evidence to Spinelli.

"All right, two teams, two cases. Team *A* is Barnes, Ramos and Finn. Team *B* is Templeton, Clarke, Spinelli and Malone. Everyone has their assignments. We'll meet back at four to get ready for the drop."

Someone knocked on the office door. Being closest, Mercedes got up and opened it. Two uniformed police officers stepped inside.

"Jeremy Barnes?" one of the officers said.

"Yes?"

"You'll need to come with us."

Chapter Eight

Stunned, Jeremy didn't know what to say. The police wanted to speak with *him?*

"I'm Max Templeton, Mr. Barnes's employer." Max took a few steps toward them, leaning on his cane. "What's this about, officer?"

The man put up his hand. "Please, sir, we've been ordered to bring Mr. Barnes to the station."

"What's the charge?" Max pushed.

"He's not being charged. The chief needs to ask him some questions."

In a daze, Jeremy walked to the door. Mercedes stepped up beside him.

The lead officer blocked her path. "Only Mr. Barnes."

"I'm his partner," she said. "He doesn't go anywhere without me."

"Or me," Bobby Finn stood.

"It's okay," Jeremy said, motioning for Bobby to sit back down.

"I'm going," Mercedes said.

"I'm sorry, ma'am, but—"

"Nothing to be sorry about." She pushed past them and opened the door. "Let's go. We've got work to do and you're using up our precious time."

The lead officer's lips set in a thin line. He was frustrated, but knew better than to argue. Jeremy actually welcomed her protective gesture.

One of the officers opened the back door to the squad car. Mercedes got in and Jeremy slid in beside her. He noticed she looked a little pale.

"You all right?" he queried.

"Sure, sure." She waved him off.

"Officer?" Jeremy said. "Why the cloak and dagger routine? Can't you tell me what this is about?"

"We were following up on a lead in the Weddle case and found some suspicious items." He glanced at the driver, then over his shoulder at Jeremy. "You'll see them when we get to the station. The chief wants to conduct the interview."

"Have I been implicated in a crime?" He wondered if that was his stalker's new strategy.

"No, sir. Not directly."

Jeremy glanced at Mercedes, who was deep in concentration. Or was she having some kind of anxiety attack?

"Mercedes?"

She didn't answer, just stared out the window.

She'd balled her hand into a fist between them. He

placed his hand over it to comfort her. She didn't look at him, didn't seem to notice the touch.

They drove a few more blocks in silence, Jeremy trying to make sense of the latest development.

The officer parked behind an old brick house. The second officer opened Mercedes's door and she practically sprung from the car. Jeremy followed and they went into the back entrance of the police station.

"Please wait here," the lead officer said, opening a door to a room with large table in the center.

Jeremy and Mercedes sat on the far side of the table.

"We'll get the chief," the officer said, and shut the door.

"Think they locked it?" he asked, half joking.

"Very funny," she muttered. She paced the interrogation room.

"What happened to you in the squad car?"

Her gorgeous brown eyes widened. "What do you mean?"

"Something was troubling you."

"I don't like police cars."

"But you were a police officer for seven years."

"Long story." She sat down and faced him. "Do you think this is about your stalker?"

"Possibly."

"Be careful how you answer them," she advised. "They have ways to make you say things to incriminate yourself."

"I know. I'm one of *them* remember?"

She sighed. "I don't like this."

"I haven't done anything wrong."

"Neither have ninety percent of the criminals we've sent to prison, or so they say."

The door opened and a rather husky man in a navy suit walked in. "I'm Chief Ivars," he said.

"Jeremy Barnes." He shook the chief's hand. "This is my partner, Mercedes Ramos. We're private investigators hired by the Weddles to help find their son."

The chief motioned for them to sit and he positioned himself across the table. "I'll be honest, Mr. Barnes. We don't like people messing with our investigation, neither does the FBI."

"I'm afraid I don't understand."

He narrowed his blue-gray eyes at Jeremy as if trying to make out his character. "We found something near Meyer's Creek that's puzzling, to say the least. We'd like to show it to you."

"Of course."

"Kyle?" the chief called.

An officer brought in an evidence bag. With gloved hands, he opened the bag and pulled out a beat-up nylon backpack.

"We're not sure what it means, so we'd like your thoughts," the chief said. He nodded to his officer.

The officer pulled a thick blue folder from the backpack. Opening it, he slipped out a piece of paper and placed it in front of Jeremy, then another and another. Jeremy's heart slammed against his chest. They were photocopies of newspaper stories revolving around SCI or Blackwell and all with Jeremy's name highlighted in yellow.

They were in sequential order, from a case dated six months ago, up until the Crimson Killer case in Chicago. Jeremy struggled with anger and rising panic. The officer pulled out the last article. The headline read, Billionaire's Son Missing.

Jeremy pushed back in his chair and paced to the window overlooking the parking lot. God, did his stalker have something to do with the boy's disappearance? A way to get Jeremy's full attention? How could he know Blackwell would take the case?

"Mr. Barnes," the chief said.

Six months ago. What case had Jeremy been working on six months ago? Had he screwed up? Sent someone to prison and a family member was out for revenge?

"Jeremy?"

He turned at the sound of Mercedes's voice. She shot him a half smile. He could tell it was forced. He was in trouble, or had caused trouble and now he'd have to expose his personal problems to the local police.

"Last night," he started, "I was lured out onto the beach and assaulted. I don't know who he was or what I've done, but he made it clear he wants me dead."

The officer looked at the chief.

"It's true," Mercedes said. "I followed him out there and saw the man try to strangle Jeremy. I scared him off."

"And what about this?" The chief motioned to his officer who placed a small photograph to the table.

Phillip.

Jeremy's blood ran cold.

He pulled out his wallet and rifled through it, but the photograph of Jeremy with his best friend, Phillip McDevish, was gone. It was staring back at him from the table.

"He took it from my wallet?" He looked at Mercedes. "Yesterday morning, when you came to get me, my room was ransacked and my wallet was open. It was him. The bastard drugged me and broke into my room. Some cash was missing, but I'd thought I'd lost track," he hesitated. "I didn't notice the photograph of Phillip and me had been taken."

"He drugged you?" the police chief said.

"He was barely able to stand yesterday morning," Mercedes confirmed. "We thought he had the flu."

She no longer thought him a drunk. Something had definitely shifted in their partnership.

"Who would do this, Mr. Barnes?" the chief asked.

He shook his head, staring at the photograph. Phillip, his best friend. The boy who'd been truly lost.

"We're working on that," Mercedes offered. "Part

of our team is looking into his old cases to figure out who's been stalking Jeremy."

"Do you have any leads on who owns the backpack?" Jeremy asked.

"We've dusted everything inside for prints, no matches yet," the chief said. "In the meantime, we think it's best if you keep your distance from the Weddle case. We don't need the complications."

Jeremy clenched his jaw and nodded. It was a reasonable request. But a boy was lost and needed him and he couldn't do a thing about it. Just like—

"No problem, sir," Mercedes said. "We've got plenty of other cases for Agent Barnes to work on."

What in the queen's name was she talking about?

"There's something else." Ivars pulled a diary from the backpack. "There are notes in here about the Weddle case. Is it yours?"

Jeremy eyed the leather-bound diary. "No."

"Your name is scribbled in a few spots, along with itineraries, train schedules. Something about a tube."

"The public transport system in London," Jeremy said. "He's definitely British, in which case you'll want to connect with Scotland Yard to match fingerprints. I've got contacts there if you need them."

"Good. Kyle, get him a pair of gloves," the chief ordered, then addressed Jeremy. "Why don't you look through the journal, see if you can make sense of it."

They shook hands. "Take your time. My deputy will ask a few more questions, take an official statement and then you're free to go."

"Thank-you," Jeremy said.

Ivars left the diary, but packed up the rest of the evidence, including the photograph of Jeremy and Phillip. Jeremy started to object, wanting it back. But it was evidence that might lead to the stalker or the kidnapper. Could he be one in the same? Jeremy couldn't stand the fact he might be responsible for the boy's kidnapping.

"I will not let him ruin my case," he muttered.

"It's not just your case," Mercedes said. "And you should be more worried about saving your butt, don't you think?"

"Why do you care about my *butt* all of the sudden?" he asked.

The officer returned with a pair of gloves and left them alone. Jeremy paged through the diary, Mercedes looking over his shoulder.

"Look at this." He pointed to a page about the Crimson Killer. "It's as if he were trying to solve the case."

"Or he's the killer."

Jeremy glanced into her brown eyes. "The killer was a woman."

"Your stalker could be a woman."

"What, the bloke that pinned me to the sand?"

"Good point." She studied the diary. "So, he's

stalking you and trying to solve your cases, like he's trying to prove something."

"I thought he simply hated me and wanted me dead."

"No, not dead. He wants something more than that."

"What?"

"He wants to make you squirm."

THEY SPENT THE MORNING going through the journal, answering questions and making an official statement.

Mercedes should be resentful that she'd lost four hours at the police department with Jeremy, but she wasn't. Jeremy's situation was serious and she knew the rest of the Blackwell team had to be focused on finding Lucas.

When they returned to the Command Center, they updated Max on the materials found by police. He assigned Jeremy and Mercedes the chore of going through Barnes's old case files to uncover leads to the stalker's identity.

"I'm sorry you got dragged into this," Jeremy said across the desk from her.

She glanced up from the file in her hand. She noticed an edge to his usually controlled demeanor.

"It's not your fault," she said. "Besides, I want to help."

"Why?"

"Why not? I mean, why are you always so defensive?"

"Look who's talking," he said.

"Yeah, so I'm an expert on being defensive so I know when you're being defensive."

"I'm not used to relying on people," he admitted.

"Me, neither."

"We have something in common."

"Seems like it." It suddenly struck her that they *were* very alike in some ways—independent and stubborn. But that's where it ended. This man worked from a place of extreme control and detachment.

In her early twenties Mercedes realized that if you were detached, you didn't feel anything at all, including the good stuff. You might as well be dead.

Although a reserved man, Jeremy had opened up last night after the attack and again this morning when he'd eyed the photograph of the two boys. Yet he hadn't shown much emotion when she'd accidentally kissed him last night. That whole episode had been freakin' weird. It was as if her head had moved against her will.

Dios mio! Maybe Mami was right. Maybe Mercedes's clock was ticking and she needed a man. But work wasn't the place to find one.

She glanced at Jeremy who studied a document in his hand. For someone in such control, she'd seen incredible sadness in his eyes when he'd looked at the photograph of the two boys.

"Who was that boy in the photograph?" she asked.

"What, you didn't recognize me?"

"I did, although you've changed." Boy had he. The kid in the photo was skinny and goofy looking. Nothing like the handsome, refined man who sat across the desk from her.

"Who was the other boy?"

Jeremy took a deep breath. "His name was Phillip."

"Was?"

"We were best friends in grade school."

"And?"

"And nothing. We lost touch."

She sensed there was more to it. "If I'm going to help you I need to know things, like why the stalker would steal that photograph from your wallet. Why not your credit cards?"

"I don't know."

"Tell me about Phillip. Maybe there's a connection."

"There isn't."

"You sure?"

He didn't answer. Instead, he glanced through some papers.

She wasn't going to push, but it really would help her to know as much as possible about his life, his career…his loves.

Well, maybe not his loves.

"It was eighth grade," he started. "We were in the

park playing football. Mum didn't like me playing football because she thought I'd get all bloody."

"Aw, she was worried about you, how sweet."

"She was afraid I'd bleed on her carpet."

He'd said it so matter-of-factly. Yet he had to be hurt by his mother caring more about carpeting than her son.

She studied his profile but couldn't get a read on what he was feeling.

"Phillip and I were kicking around a football when these older boys came by wanting to join in. Phillip and I weren't easy with people, more the awkward types," he glanced at her. "I know you find that hard to believe."

She smiled.

"Anyway, the other boys started playing rough. I couldn't come home all bloody, so I told Phillip we should leave. But he liked the attention from the older boys. I begged Phillip to leave with me. They started calling me names, Phillip joined in, so I left. About seven that evening his mum rang our house wanting to know where he was. I told her he'd stayed at the park with some friends. She asked why I'd left him. I said I'd had homework."

"You lied?"

"I didn't want to appear to be a bad friend, which in retrospect, I was."

"You couldn't force him to leave the park with you."

He shrugged. "He turned up the next morning, said he'd spent the night at one of the boys' houses. Things were never the same after that."

"You weren't cool enough to hang out with him?"

"I thought so at first, but Phillip had this strange look in his eye after that night. He avoided me for some other reason, shame, maybe? He turned into a smart aleck, hung out with unsavory types, talked back to teachers, that kind of thing. A year later his family moved away."

"Sounds like adolescent stuff to me."

"Whatever it was, he never recovered. I found out a few years ago that he'd gone the drug route, got hooked on something. Devastated his family. I think he was self-medicating because of what happened that night."

"You don't know that for sure," she said. "And even so, it's not your fault."

He placed the papers to the desk and stared her down. "If I'd been a true friend, I never would have left him. I know what it feels like when someone abandons you. What was I thinking?"

"You were thirteen," she consoled.

"That's no excuse." He tapped a pen against the desk. "He was my best friend."

And possibly the only person who understood this guy, Mercedes thought. He was a complex one, so in control, yet so loyal to someone who'd ended their friendship to be with cooler kids.

"You know what really bothers me?" he asked.

"Bad wine?"

He eyed her. "Friends who aren't true friends; like the Reynolds boy. Shayne Lynk said he was bullying Lucas, telling him he was a baby because he depended on his parents for everything. That's not a friend."

A few minutes passed, Mercedes studying her partner as he reviewed a case file.

"Hello," he said, his gaze locking on something in the file.

"What?" She walked around the desk to look over his shoulder. He studied a photograph of a middle-aged man.

"Who's that?"

"Wayne Gibson," Jeremy said. "Four years ago, he was convicted of arson for hire, but we suspected his big brother orchestrated the crime. Big brother cornered me one night and said Wayne was innocent. I said if he knew who did it, to come forward. He wouldn't implicate himself, so little brother went to prison."

"Why do you think he'd go to the trouble of finding you now?"

"Help me go through this file, will you?"

He handed her some papers and their fingers touched, setting off a spark of awareness that made her wary. She'd been so good at keeping an emotional distance from partners since the early heartbreak at the Chicago PD. What was so different about Jeremy Barnes?

She went to her side of the desk. The reserved Englishman intrigued her, she admitted. Not only his intelligence, but his compassion and maybe even his vulnerability, drew her in. Other men were always so good at dismissing her as beautiful—fun to play with, but not take seriously. Jeremy was the first partner who treated her as an equal.

"What am I looking for?" She analyzed the stack of police notes.

"Anything about the Gibson family that might be relevant. Maybe something happened to Wayne in prison and that's why his brother is after me."

She glanced at the wall clock. It read four. She and Jeremy had been at it all afternoon, while the rest of the team was readying for the ransom drop. A part of her wanted to get out of here and do what she came to do—prove her skills by helping find a missing boy.

"Mercedes?"

"Yes?"

"Go on and help the team. I'll be fine."

"No, I can't." What should she say? She'd been assigned by Max to be Barnes's babysitter.

The truth was, staying with him had less to do with Max Templeton's order and more to do with wanting to help Jeremy.

"I'm second in command," he said. "What if I order you to go?"

"We're partners. I'll stay."

He leaned forward in his chair. "Neither of us wants this partnership."

His comment stung. She'd started to feel a kinship with the man, but by the tone of his voice he didn't feel the same way. Still, something held her back.

"Stop talking so much and focus on the files," she snapped.

"Okay, partner, on one condition. You tell me why you get so jumpy in the back of a police car."

"It's nothing." She waved him off.

"Mercedes?" he pushed.

Loving the sound of her name spoken with an English accent, she glanced at him, his blue eyes penetrating her resolve to keep this secret to herself.

"I was twelve. I got arrested."

"Excuse me?"

"My big brothers were vandalizing an old warehouse. I was following them to get them in trouble. But it backfired and they got away. I got caught with the spray paint because I grabbed the evidence to bring home to Mami and Papi." She leaned back in her chair. "I'll never forget that sick feeling in my stomach. Kids in the neighborhood were outside when the police brought me home. They all swarmed the car to get a good look at the criminal. It was horrible. But I did get inspired."

"Not to pursue a life of crime?"

"To become a cop. Officer Susan Tumwater was

one of the arresting officers. I'll never forget how everyone looked at her, with such respect. Even Papi."

"What happened to your brothers?"

"Nothing. I never told on them. They already had been in trouble with police. I was afraid if they were caught they'd go away, to jail."

"And you didn't want them to go away?"

"Stupid, huh? I ruined my reputation to get them in trouble and then I take the fall for their crime."

"Why did you want to get them in trouble?"

"It's a brother-sister thing."

He shot her a puzzled look.

"The boys always got the most attention. My sister and I were expected to cook and clean up after the men. It was like being a second-class citizen. I resented that. I wanted the same kind of attention the boys got."

The same kind of respect.

"What happened after your arrest?" he asked.

"I had to do community service. It was okay, though. I worked with little kids, so I didn't mind. It got me out of the house. I had even considered becoming a teacher.

"Really?"

"Don't sound so shocked. The kids liked me."

"I'll bet they did."

"You're making fun of me."

He put his folder down and leaned forward. "No,

I'm not. You have a confident air about you that would make children feel secure. And you have a sense of humor."

She'd gotten a sense of humor from growing up in a large family. She felt badly that Jeremy had missed out on that sibling connection.

Even though she resented her brothers, she couldn't imagine life without them.

"So Phillip was like your brother?" she asked.

"I guess you could say that."

And he'd lost him at thirteen.

"What about the rest of your childhood?"

He looked up through his rimless glasses. "I don't remember having a childhood."

She found herself wanting to reach across the desk and touch his cheek, ease the pain from his eyes.

"Come on, I told you my story."

"Parents divorced when I was ten. Didn't see my father much after that."

"What about your mom?"

"She was too obsessed with herself to be bothered with her son." He flipped another page in his folder.

"But you had friends, right?"

"Only Phillip. I was an intelligent child, two grades ahead. I was picked on because of my looks." His eyes roamed a sheet of paper as if he were reading her the weather report. "The only time I got parental attention was when I told my father I wanted to become a solicitor. Suddenly he took great interest in me, helping me plan my curriculum and my career. That ended when I dropped the bomb that I was going to be an investigator, not an attorney."

"What changed your mind?"

"I realized I wasn't studying law for myself, but rather to earn my father's love and respect." He turned another sheet of paper over. "He didn't have it to give."

She could relate. She'd always hoped her father would come around and give her the respect she deserved.

"Getting pregnant with me was a manipulation on my mother's part," he continued. "She thought giving Edward a child would keep them married and her in expensive jewelry. It didn't make a bit of difference. He abandoned us and she was stuck with me."

"I'm sorry."

"It's life. Nothing to be sorry about. It taught me I shouldn't have children."

Her breath caught. She couldn't imagine a life without kids. "What? Why?"

"With Elizabeth and Edward as role models? I wouldn't know the first thing about parenting a child."

"You shouldn't be so hard on yourself."

He didn't answer, just eyed the file on the desk. "Blast," he swore.

"What?"

He glanced at her. "Wayne Gibson died in a prison fight."

"That puts his brother as number one stalker suspect," she said.

The door burst open and Bobby Finn raced to Jeremy's desk. "You'll never believe it, guv," he said, out of breath.

"Calm down, Bobby. What's happened?"

"The ransom drop was muddled by some teenager. He says he's your son."

Chapter Nine

"My son?" Jeremy said, pushing to his feet. "What kind of rubbish is that?"

"I know, guv. It's outrageous. They've got him in custody. Templeton wants you to come down to the police station."

"What about the ransom drop?" Mercedes asked.

"Botched. The cops thought the teenager was the perpetrator and followed him. They arrested him, but he didn't have the money. Either he's not their man or he passed it off to an accomplice. He won't talk to the Feds or locals. He said he'd only speak with Jeremy Barnes. C'mon, guv, the car's out front."

Jeremy automatically straightened the pile of folders on his desk and headed out with Bobby and Mercedes. What was the bloke's angle? Drive Jeremy completely insane by claiming to be a son he didn't have? After all, it was impossible.

"How old is the boy?" he asked, getting into the back seat of the car. Mercedes got in beside him.

"He won't tell us, but he seems in the eighteen-to-twenty-year-old range."

"You were a teenager yourself that many years ago," Mercedes calculated. "Your stalker is putting you through the wringer."

That was the truth. An illegitimate son popping up after all these years would make Jeremy question more than the means of the child's conception. It would make him question his entire life. Jeremy was a responsible sort, not one to have mindless, unprotected sex.

"Is he American?" Jeremy asked, hopeful.

"No, guv, English. Sounds working class to me."

"And what do they know about him so far?"

"Nothing. Like I said, he's not talking." Bobby glanced at them through the rearview mirror. "He's a clever one, guv. He knows enough about the law to keep his mouth shut and ask for an attorney."

"So he didn't just ask for me, he asked for an attorney, as well?"

"Yes, but the Feds are taking their time to see if they can get anything out of him first. Since it's a small town, they told him it would take a while to find him representation. Not much criminal action in a tourist town like this."

"Any word on the Weddle boy?" Jeremy asked.

"No, sir."

Jeremy's mind raced. If he'd put the boy in danger because of a personal vendetta…

Mercedes touched his shoulder. "Stop it."

She knew what he was thinking, bloody hell, she could read his feelings, something no other human being had been able to do. He glanced out his window. He'd worked so hard to keep his feelings and thoughts hidden from everyone around him. It had been the best way to emotionally protect himself from people who were supposed to love him. Yet somehow this female could see through his protective layers. Not good. He didn't want to be that exposed to anyone.

They pulled up to the police station and got out. Templeton met Jeremy on the sidewalk.

"They won't let us in," Max said. "It's up to you. Find out what you can. I'm sending Bobby back with Joe and Eddie to continue working on leads. Cassie and I will stay here and wait until you're finished."

Jeremy nodded and started up the front steps. Mercedes walked alongside him.

"You should stay with Max and Cassie," he said.

She ignored him.

They were greeted by two men in uniform and two in suits. Federal officers.

"Jeremy Barnes?" A man in a suit stepped forward.

"Yes, sir."

"I'm Agent Timmons with the FBI." They shook hands. "My team is working with the local police on the Weddle investigation. We've got a man in custody that claims he's your son. He's downstairs in lockup." He glanced at Mercedes. "You'll have to stay here."

"I'm his partner."

"I'm sorry, ma'am."

"Look, I'm on loan from the FBI. I know there's no reason why I can't accompany him downstairs so let's go."

She stared him down. That look of determination would make a criminal confess.

They headed down a steep flight of stairs into a musty basement. Timmons led them down a short hallway with a cell at the end. A man lay on a cot, wedged in the corner, his face to the wall. The suspect wore beat-up jeans and a denim jacket. Jeremy noticed a rip across the bottom.

"Get up, kid," Timmons ordered.

The suspect didn't move.

"I said, get up." Timmons unlocked the door, grabbed the kid from behind and jerked him to his feet. "We don't have time for games. We got Mr. Barnes like you asked. Now, where's the boy?"

The man turned around and Jeremy's breath slammed against his chest. He looked so bloody familiar. Where had he seen him before?

He was a young man, at most twenty years old, with angular features, blue eyes and a narrow face. But it was something about his expression that haunted Jeremy.

"What, no warm greetings?" the boy taunted, looking at Jeremy.

"Do I know you?"

The young man laughed, a hollow, sad sound. Jeremy crossed his arms over his chest and leaned against the wall. For some reason, this punk's attitude disturbed Jeremy more than it should.

"Nah, don't worry, mate," the boy said. "You don't know me."

"Then what's this about? Why involve me in the kidnapping?"

"Oh, I had nothing to do with that." He sat back on the cot and studied his fingernails.

"What were you doing at the wine shop?" Agent Timmons said.

"I was hoping to get a few minutes with me dad, is all." He glanced up at Jeremy and smiled.

"I do not have a son. You have me mixed up with someone else."

"Do I?"

"Enough of this," Timmons said. "I brought you Barnes, now tell us what you know about the Weddle case."

He glanced at Timmons, then back to Jeremy. "I know a lot." He leaned forward, "See, I'm smart like me father. Actually, smarter, if you wanna know the God's honest truth."

"Yeah, how do you figure that?" Timmons said.

"I got him out to the beach and gave him a right scare, didn't I, guv?"

"It was you who attacked me last night?" Jeremy demanded.

The young man smiled, pleased with himself.

"We'll add assault to the charges," Timmons threatened.

"Who sent you?" Jeremy said.

"No one sent me. I come all by me self. Wanted a family reunion. If you're wondering about Mum, well, she doesn't know I'm here. She wouldn't care anyway. She's busy with her new family, Robert and the girls."

"We don't care about all that. Tell us what you know about the Weddle case," Timmons demanded, pulling out a notebook.

"Not you. Him." He pointed at Jeremy.

"He's just a civilian."

"Are you gonna let him talk to you like that?" he asked Jeremy. "You're more spineless than I thought."

"Listen, kid," Timmons said. "We can do this the easy way or the hard way. A little boy is missing so rules are nonexistent, if you catch my drift."

The young man laughed again. An ache filled Jeremy's chest. What was it about this boy that unnerved him? Was he too much of a reminder of Jeremy at his age? Angry, determined and hurt? More importantly, what made him come all the way across the world to find Jeremy?

"Ah, I know enough about me dad to know he wouldn't let you beat up an innocent man," the boy said, eyeing Jeremy. "His son he could care less about but an innocent civilian is another story."

Timmons took a step toward him, but Jeremy stopped him with a hand to his shoulder. “Can I have a word?”

Timmons locked the cell and they went to the stairs. “I was with Scotland Yard for more than ten years,” Jeremy said. “Let me have a run at him.”

“I don’t like it.”

“It’s the quickest way to get information. He wants to play games with me, let him play.”

“We’ll be upstairs listening on the intercom.”

Jeremy started back to the cell and Mercedes followed. “Go upstairs,” Jeremy said.

“Let’s not fight about that again. Where you go, I go. Let’s find out what this kid is about.”

They went back to the cell.

“Is this your girlfriend?” He looked at Mercedes. “Better watch it, he’s not exactly the responsible type. He’ll get you pregnant and leave you with the baby.”

“What’s your name?” Jeremy asked.

“Why?” The kid eyed him.

“I’m trying to be polite.”

“What’s her name?” He winked at Mercedes.

“Mercedes Ramos,” she said.

“Andrew Burke, nice to meet you, Miss. I’d kiss your hand, but me dad might think I’m making a move on his girl.” With hands interlaced behind his head, he leaned against the wall.

“Let’s put the whole father-son issue aside for a

moment," Jeremy said. "What do you know about the Weddle case?"

"I know the ransom's a fake. No one's got that boy."

"Really? And you know this how?" Mercedes quizzed.

"I'm psychic."

"You're going to be charged with kidnapping and extortion if you don't start cooperating," Jeremy reminded him. "Doesn't that bother you?"

The boy's gaze drifted from admiring Mercedes to glaring at Jeremy. "What bothers me are fathers abandoning their sons. What bothers me is being forgotten, like the Weddle boy. He was forgotten, but he wasn't kidnapped. No, that's another crime altogether."

"Do you know who made the ransom demand?"

"Whoever it is, he's not your kidnapper. He just wants money. He's probably going to lose his house, or worse, the love of his life. That would make a man steal, wouldn't it, maybe even kill?"

"Why are you here?" Jeremy demanded.

"What, in jail? I still don't know that, me self. I'm trying to help, is all."

"Why?"

"To contribute to society," he mocked.

"That's rubbish."

Andrew jumped to his feet and grabbed the bars. Mercedes took a step back. Jeremy didn't budge. He kept eye contact with the boy.

"I came to prove I'm smarter than you, my dear father. I'm smarter, I'm better and you're nothing but a fumbling fool. I did pretty good up to now."

"How's that?"

He squeezed the bars. "I had the controlled, intelligent Inspector Barnes coming apart at the seams, didn't I? The mousetrap, the note, the skeleton on the beach. You were sweating it up pretty good, yeah?"

"Why?" Jeremy felt, his control slipping.

"So you'd know what it's like to have your whole life crumble into pieces at your feet." His blue eyes radiated hatred.

"What happened to you?" Jeremy whispered.

"I woke up one day and discovered my life was a lie. Thanks to you."

"Young man, I don't even know you."

"But you know Nancy."

Jeremy clenched his jaw and stared at him. Someone had done their homework, right down to Jeremy's Achilles heel.

Nancy. The woman who'd seduced him, made him feel loved and wanted, then left him without a word of explanation.

Jeremy turned and walked away, Mercedes right behind him.

"What, don't want to talk anymore?" Andrew called.

"Not with a liar."

"Wait, where are you going?"

"I'm done with you." He turned and stared him down from the other end of the hallway. "You've compromised this investigation. You're an arrogant punk. I'll let the federal agents have their run at you. Maybe they'll have more luck." He opened the door to the stairs.

"No, wait, Dad—Barnes. I've got something on the Weddle case that you need to see."

Jeremy closed the door and turned to him. The kid's expression had changed from cocky arrogance to genuine concern.

"What, you afraid they'll beat you to a pulp and dump your body in the ocean when they're through?" Jeremy taunted.

"I could care less about them. That boy is out there, alone. You've got to find him."

"That's news?" He reached for the door again.

"Wait, Miss, make him listen."

Mercedes placed her hand to Jeremy's shoulder. He glanced into her eyes and she nodded as if she thought the boy's plea was genuine.

"Don't tell me you're being fooled by this?" Jeremy said.

"We've got nothing to lose by listening to him."

"You listen. I'm finished."

"They didn't send a photograph or let the parents hear the boy's voice, did they?" Andrew called out. "That's because there are no kidnappers. Why not send a photograph and why wait so long to send a ransom demand? Someone is extorting money and I've got a short list on my laptop. It's in my car, by Meyer's Creek. Get me out of here and I'll show you."

The boy suddenly sounded more like an educated teenager than an ignorant punk.

Jeremy opened the door.

"He's been gone a week!" the boy shouted after him. "I can help!"

Jeremy went upstairs and was met by a group of curious agents.

"I can't get anywhere with him," Jeremy said.

"Is he your son?" Agent Timmons asked.

"I've never seen him before in my life."

He strode out of the police department to the sidewalk where Max and Cassie were waiting.

"The young man inside who claims to be my son, is also the man who's been threatening me and attacked me on the beach. I don't know why or who sent him."

"So he's not connected to the Weddle case?" Max said.

"I doubt it. He's unstable and is best kept in jail. But I don't think him capable of kidnapping a boy."

"He said something about having suspect leads on his laptop," Mercedes said.

"He's been working on this case?" Max said in disbelief.

"He claims to have leads, yes, but I'm not sure I believe him. I think he's psychotic." Jeremy glanced at the police station and back to Max. "In any case, they'll get it out of him."

"I'm not sure I like the sound of that," Cassie said.

"It's what he deserves," Jeremy shot back.

Bobby pulled up to the curb and they all climbed into the rented sedan. The drive back to the Command Center was quiet—too quiet—Mercedes thought. She wondered what Templeton thought of this development and if she should share her gut instinct that the man in the cell was, in fact, Jeremy's son.

She struggled with the concept, trying to figure out how a man like Jeremy could have conceived a child and know nothing about it. Jeremy Barnes was not the type to abandon his own son, she thought. No, not after being left by both his father and best friend.

Who was this Nancy that Andrew had mentioned? Could she have really been the mother of Jeremy's child?

She glanced at him. He stared straight ahead, his jaw clenched.

If the boy was his son, that would blow Jeremy's life to hell. What had the boy said, that he wanted his father to know what it felt like to have his whole life crumble into pieces? If the boy's claim was true, it would tear the honorable Jeremy Barnes apart.

She shouldn't care. Jeremy was a means to an end, a way to carve out a permanent spot on the Blackwell team.

Oh, stop lying to yourself. You kinda like the guy.

They pulled up to the Command Center and Jeremy jumped out, making his way to the office. It was almost as if shame drove him away from the rest of them. Did a part of him sense the truth, deep down in his heart?

Max motioned for Cassie to go inside, leaving Mercedes and Max standing just outside the door.

"Agent Ramos, what do you make of it?" he asked.

She sighed. "I don't think Andrew is involved in the Weddle kidnapping. He said Lucas wasn't kidnapped but he thinks someone is exploiting the situation to extort money from the family. He seems to be genuinely concerned about Lucas, as if he identifies with him somehow."

"You don't think he's crazy?"

"No, it's more like he's in pain."

"Why is he after Jeremy?"

"He says he's trying to prove that he's smarter than his dad."

"Is it possible?"

She didn't answer. What could she say? That although it didn't make rational sense, she suspected it was true?

"We need to find out everything about the young man," Max said.

"Yes, sir."

"I'll get Eddie started on some background, the

rest of us will work on the Weddle case. I need you to continue watching over Jeremy to make sure he isn't in danger."

"You make it sound as if I'm incapable of taking care of myself," Jeremy said from the office door.

She closed her eyes in dread. He'd heard them talking as if he were a victim, not a fellow agent.

"So, that was her job all along? To spy on me?"

Chapter Ten

"I asked her to keep an eye on you, yes," Max said. "I was concerned about post trauma issues."

Mercedes kept her mouth shut, not wanting to aggravate the situation.

Jeremy walked up to Max. "Don't be. I'm perfectly capable of performing my job responsibilities."

"It has nothing to do with that, mate."

"And when did we become mates?"

Max didn't answer, but she read disappointment in his eyes. Thinking they needed privacy, she took a step toward the office door.

"Stay right there," Jeremy ordered.

He glared at her, his blue eyes darker than usual, his expression controlled. "You're officially relieved of your duties as spy. Since I can't trust you, I want you off the team."

"That isn't your decision to make, Jeremy," Max said in a low voice.

"Isn't it?" He turned his attention to Max. "Remember what happened in Chicago? We agreed that members of Blackwell must be able to trust each other, implicitly?"

"Yes," Max said.

"I don't trust her."

Mercedes lost it. "Grow up, Barnes. So I was keeping an eye on you, so what? Has it occurred to you that if I hadn't been watching out for you, you could have been hit by that car or killed last night on the beach? You should be thanking me instead of trying to get me fired. I have better things to do than stand out here and argue. Lucas Weddle is still missing, remember?"

He didn't respond.

"*Ay,* you drive me crazy." She waved her hand and went into the Command Center.

She shifted behind her desk and started making notes about their interaction with Jeremy's supposed son.

"Where's Templeton?" Bobby Finn asked walking over to his desk.

"Arguing with Barnes outside."

Cassie walked up to Mercedes. "Is the boy really Jeremy's son?"

"Not much of a boy. He's at least eighteen," Mercedes said. "Barnes denies it, but you have to ask yourself why Andrew would go to all that trouble, stalking him and setting up that scene on the beach. The kid's got one helluva grudge."

"But Jeremy was never married," Cassie said.

"You don't have to be." No, Mercedes's older brother got his girlfriend pregnant before marrying her.

"Listen up," Max said, walking into the room. "This case is still hot, the stakes are up and a boy remains missing."

Barnes followed closely behind and positioned himself a few feet away from Max. Jeremy crossed his arms over his chest and leaned against a support beam. He didn't look at Mercedes. He was obviously still angry.

She'd saved his butt last night. Didn't that count for something?

Ah, chica, not when a man's pride is wounded. He probably thought she'd followed him around because she admired his keen investigative sense. She knew it irked him that she was following orders, that she wasn't connected to him by choice.

But then that wasn't entirely true, was it?

"The new development is about Jeremy's stalker, who we think is the same man they took into custody. Jeremy?" Max stepped aside.

Jeremy uncrossed his arms. "As you may have heard, the young man says he's my son. I've never been married, nor do I have a son, so this is impossible. We need to determine the man's angle and his involvement in the Weddle boy's disappearance."

"The boy's name?" Eddie asked.

"Andrew. Andrew Burke. From England."

"Doesn't ring any bells, guv?" Bobby asked.

"None," Jeremy said. "No old cases, no enemies, nothing."

"Why's he messing with the investigation?" Spinelli asked.

"The boy says he's trying to outsmart his father," Mercedes offered. "In other words, he's trying to solve our case to prove he's better than Jeremy." She glanced at him. He still hadn't looked at her.

"Sounds like he's off his trolley," Bobby said.

Then a thought struck Mercedes. "Maybe not. What if he's telling the truth?"

Jeremy shot her a furious look.

"Hear me out," she said. "At Quantico I took a class on profiling serial criminals. It's possible that Andrew thinks, for whatever reason, that Jeremy *is* his father and he's going to show him up by solving this case. These criminals can be mentally ill, but brilliant, which means he may actually have something legitimate on the investigation."

"Impossible," Jeremy said.

She ignored him. "When we were leaving lockup, he called out two things. First, that Lucas Weddle had been gone for days before the ransom request. Why wait?" She glanced at each team member.

"And two?" Spinelli asked.

He was buying into her theory. Good, she had an ally. "The second point—why weren't the parents given proof the boy is still alive? Why weren't they allowed to hear his voice, or see a photo of him holding the daily paper? Because maybe the kidnapper and the ransom demand are not connected. Andrew mentioned having a short list of extortion suspects on his laptop."

"He's bloody insane," Bobby scoffed.

"I agree," Jeremy said.

Max shifted on his cane. "Agent Ramos, what do you think?"

She took a deep breath, held Jeremy's gaze and said, "Instinct tells me he's not insane. I think there's more to it and it's worth pursuing."

"Too late," Spinelli said. "The feds won't let us get close again."

"Not necessarily true," Mercedes said. "He hasn't been formally charged with anything and my guess is they'll have to let him talk to his father." She glanced at Jeremy.

His eyes narrowed and the room went silent.

She'd been waiting years to be respected enough to be asked for her opinion, a theory, and with this team she finally had her chance.

She glanced at Max. Was he going to fire her because he assigned her a task that broke trust among team members? More importantly, was he going to write off her opinion about Andrew Burke?

"She's right," Max said.

"What the bloody hell—"

Max cut off Jeremy's objections. "It's a solid lead.

We've been at this for days and we're no closer to finding the boy. This Andrew Burke development could be something." He turned to Mercédes. "Why did they bring him in?"

"He was seen hanging around the wine shop. He actually went inside and used the bathroom so they figured he was their man. But when they caught up to him, he didn't have the money."

"So our friend, Andrew, could be a diversion," Max suggested.

"You mean he's working with the real kidnappers?" Bobby asked.

"It's a possibility," Max said. "Although why is he involving Barnes?"

"That's easy," Spinelli offered. "He bypasses the Feds."

"We're his direct link to the Weddles," Max said. "Clever."

"So he dreams up the story about being related to Barnes so he can work the ransom angle directly with the Weddles through us?" Eddie questioned.

"But why stalk Jeremy?" Mercedes asked. "Why attack him on the beach? Something still doesn't fit."

"That's for you and Barnes to figure out," Max said. "What other developments do we have? Eddie, anything from the boy's computer?"

"Not yet, but I found some threatening e-mails in the father's trash. When I asked him about it, he said he deletes anything from an address he doesn't recognize. I didn't catch it the first time around."

"Do you think he could have received a ransom demand days ago but didn't open the e-mail?" Jeremy queried.

"Definitely possible," Eddie said. "I'm going to keep working on the father's computer, then go at the kid's again."

"Bobby, work with him on e-mail related leads," Max said.

"Pardon me, guv, I thought you wanted me watching over Agent Barnes."

His choice of words couldn't have been worse, Mercedes thought.

"New assignments," Max said. "I think if we focus on the computers we'll find a lead. Next, Agent Spinelli, find out what went wrong at the drop. Go to the wine shop and try to make sense of it. Talk to the shop owner, ask about unusual customers, odd moments, things like that."

"Yes, sir."

"Oh, I almost forgot," Eddie interrupted, looking at Mercedes. "I have a hit on the plate number you called in."

"Plate number?" Max said.

"The car that nearly hit Jeremy yesterday," Mercedes explained.

"Our friend, Mr. Burke?" Max asked.

"I'm assuming," Mercedes said.

"See if you can find his laptop," Max directed. "You'll either find evidence of the next ransom demand, or he's telling the truth and has information about the case."

"He's not telling the truth," Jeremy blurted out.

It was the first time Mercedes saw him lose his composure. She knew, by the expression on his face, that he hadn't meant to say it out loud.

"That's it, then," Max said. "Let's check back at nine this evening."

Mercedes went to Eddie and got the information about the car.

"Agent Ramos," Max called. "A moment in my office?"

She held her breath. This was it. He was going to let her go so he could keep his number two guy happy.

She went into his office and closed the door. She didn't sit down. A second later Jeremy joined them.

Trying to tamp down her anger, she crossed her arms over her chest and waited.

"I knew partnering you with Barnes would have its challenges," Max said. "I'm sorry if I made matters worse by ordering you to deceive him."

But I wasn't deceiving him. I wanted to keep him safe because...I started to care about him.

Oh, sure, if she said that out loud she'd lose her job for sure. And her self-respect.

"To that end, let's agree on no more deception."

He glanced at Jeremy. “I’m asking you to remain partners with Agent Ramos because I think your investigative styles complement each other. I also sense you’ve developed a rapport.” He glanced at Mercedes. “Am I right?”

“Yes, sir.”

She was amazed at this man’s insight and even more amazed that she wasn’t being pushed out of Blackwell.

“I don’t suppose I have any say in this?” Jeremy asked.

She held her breath.

“Please.” Max invited him to share his thoughts.

Jeremy looked directly at her. “I think you’re a sharp agent with great potential.”

She steeled herself against his next words.

“I wish you,” he glanced at Max, “both of you would have been upfront about your concerns instead of working behind my back.”

“We talked about that outside,” Max said.

“Yes, and you explained some things that I didn’t understand before.”

Mercedes was dying to know what *things* he referred to.

Jeremy pinned her with his now warm blue eyes. “I’d like to give it another try but only if I have your promise that you have no ulterior motive other than to help find Lucas.”

“That’s why I’m here,” she said.

"I need you to promise complete honesty from this point on."

"I can do that."

"Brilliant," Max said. "Get to it, then."

"Yes, sir," Mercedes headed for the door and Jeremy opened it. This time she welcomed the gesture and nodded her thanks.

Something had changed about him in the last half hour. Something big. It was as if a piece of protective armor had been peeled away from his chest. She suspected that giving up that kind of protection had to be terrifying for a man who thrived on control.

They went outside. "Back to the police station?" she asked.

"No, let's find the boy's car. He said the laptop was inside."

She noticed he didn't call the teenager by name. They'd have to deal with that issue sooner than later—the possibility of Andrew being Jeremy's son. Something didn't add up.

"Why not go back to the police station and confront him again?" she said.

Why, indeed. Jeremy took a deep breath and admitted to himself that he didn't want to see the boy, not so soon after the crushing accusation about Jeremy being his father.

It wasn't possible, yet a heavy sense of dread filled Jeremy's chest. He didn't like surprises and this turn of events was outrageously unpredictable.

"We'll give the boy some space and let the Feds do their bit to scare him," Jeremy said. "By the time we return, he'll be ready to tell us his life story."

"Hmm. Smart man."

"Glad you think so."

A few minutes of silence passed as they drove to the park. "I'm assuming his car is the little blue one that nearly ran me down."

"Someone should give him a lecture about his driving," she said.

"He was *trying* to hit me, remember?"

What could Jeremy have possibly done to make the boy hate him so much? He wasn't the boy's father; it wasn't possible. He'd been careful his whole adult life, careful and responsible.

"Listen, I *am* sorry about spying on you," she said.

"You were following orders."

"Thanks for not getting me fired."

Which would have been terribly unprofessional and unlike Jeremy. But his emotions were scrambled. To think he'd nearly insisted they lose an excellent agent because Max had been concerned about Jeremy.

She was excellent in many ways, including her ability to see past the evidence and take in the whole picture. Yes, she had great potential, this one.

Too bad she didn't have potential in other areas, as well. No, he'd never open his heart like that again, especially not with a woman who he knew wanted a family some day. He didn't begrudge her that desire. He actually admired it.

Family. He could tell Max and Cassie were headed in that direction. It might be tough to keep a family together in this line of work, but if two people loved each other enough, they could make it happen.

They pulled into the lot by Meyer's Creek. He spotted a blue compact car with a flag of Great Britain on the radio antenna.

"That's the plate number," she said eyeing the car.

She pulled over and they got out. "It's an older model so I should be able to jimmy open the door," she offered. "You'll bail me out if I get arrested?"

He shot her a half smile. She had a way of easing his tension in the worst of situations.

Glancing through the windows, he noticed a pile of clothes, empty soft drink cans, a pillow and blanket. Good God, had the boy had been sleeping in his car?

She got a long metal device from her car and slipped it inside the driver's window. He spotted a couple walking toward them wearing concerned expressions.

"My wife locked the keys in the car again," he explained. The couple nodded their sympathy and walked past.

"Your wife?" She raised an eyebrow and jerked on the metal device. The door unlocked.

He went to the passenger side and opened the door. The car wasn't dirty, exactly, just messy.

"Here." She tossed him a pair of latex gloves.

He put them on and sorted through folders, magazines and old newspapers.

"Got it!" Mercedes said.

She slipped a laptop out from underneath the front seat.

He opened the glove box and found the car's registration, which read Andrew Brown. "He may be using an alias, or many aliases." He pulled out a pouch and opened it, fearing he'd find drugs.

Why do you care what he's into?

Instead, he found various photographs of Andrew, a razor blade and a handful of driver's licenses—not his.

"He's been making fake IDs," He glanced at Mercedes. "Why? He's into something illegal?"

"Maybe we'll find answers on the laptop. Let's go."

Jeremy closed the glove box and glanced once more around the car. He noticed something sticking out from of the visor and flipped it down. A few slips of paper and credit cards drifted to the seat. He turned over a credit card. It read Nancy Burke.

Nancy. Coincidence?

Mercedes plucked a photograph from the pile of items. "Wow, cute picture."

She handed it to him and his breath caught at the sight of Nancy, the love of his life, holding a small child in her arms.

It couldn't be. His hand trembled.

"You know her?" Mercedes said.

"Yes."

"Who is she?"

He ignored her question and pulled out his mobile. He punched in Eddie's number.

"Malone," he answered.

"It's Barnes. Run a search on a credit card number for me, will you?"

"Sure, shoot."

Jeremy read him off the number.

"Whatcha lookin' for?" Eddie asked.

"Home phone number."

"Give me a minute."

Jeremy closed the door and leaned against the car. *Get ahold of yourself. This isn't possible. It's just a way for your enemy to rattle your brain, throw you off guard.*

He struggled to think of whom he'd wronged so deeply that they'd rip open his past and torture him with it.

"Okay, Robert and Nancy Burke," Eddie said. "I've got a number in England."

"Continue." He pulled out his notebook and jotted down the number. "Thanks."

"What's going on?" Mercedes said.

"Hopefully, just another one of Mr. Burke's games."

He punched in the number, realizing it was the middle of the night back home. He couldn't wait.

It rang four times.

"Hello?" a man answered.

"Nancy Burke, please. I'm calling from the United States. It's an emergency."

"Who is this?"

"Jeremy Barnes."

"Jeremy, who?"

There was a rustling sound, then, "Jeremy?" a woman said. "Oh, my God, he found you."

Chapter Eleven

"He found me? You mean—"

"He's your son, Jeremy."

"Good God, Nancy, what have you done?" he said.

"Now, wait a minute, it takes two people to create a child."

"A child I knew nothing about until I met him in a jail cell this afternoon."

"He's in jail?" she shrieked. "Oh, my God, what happened?"

"He's been brought in for questioning." He paced toward the creek and back to the car.

"For what? He couldn't have done anything wrong."

"You don't know that, Nancy."

"I know he's a good boy. He's smart and responsible and he'd never break the law."

"Nancy, hold on—start at the beginning. He's my son?"

He nodded to Mercedes and they got into the car. The Weddle case was still the priority, no matter what personal crisis he was dealing with.

"Yes, Andrew is your son. He didn't know that until about six months ago. He got into a huge argument with his father and Robert let it slip."

"His father, you mean his stepfather?"

"Robert has been Andrew's father since he was a baby."

"Yes, but I'm the boy's biological father," Jeremy confirmed.

"You are."

"Why didn't you tell me?"

"Because I was afraid you'd demand we get married and let's face it, Jeremy, we weren't marriage material."

Pain sliced through his chest. "Why?"

"Does it matter after nearly twenty years?"

"It matters when you tell me I have a son, a boy who's gone to great lengths to find me."

"I told him it was a bad idea, that you didn't want anything to do with him."

"How could you say that?"

"I didn't want him to be hurt," she said.

"You mean you didn't want him to know you'd lied to him all these years."

"I'd do anything to protect my son."

"From me?"

"From everything. We have a great life. Robert is

an excellent father and loves Andrew like his own. There was no need for him to know the truth."

"Nancy, listen to yourself."

"I did it for you, Jeremy, and for Andrew."

"Bollocks! You did it because you didn't want your son finding out his precious mummy slept with a man five years younger and broke his heart by disappearing on him."

Blast, did he really just say that? He couldn't help himself. He was bloody furious.

They pulled up to the Command Center. Mercedes motioned that she was taking the laptop inside.

"Nancy?" he said.

Silence. God, she couldn't have hung up. There was so much to say, so many unanswered questions.

"I'm sorry," she said. "I didn't know I broke your heart. I thought it was silly fun for you, too."

Jeremy's one experience with what he thought was true love.

And the woman referred to it as silly fun.

Taking a deep breath, he said in a tired voice, "It was a long time ago, Nancy. You and I are different people now."

"How does Andrew look?" she asked.

"He looks...like you." He suddenly realized why the boy seemed so familiar.

"Except for his eyes. He has your radiant eyes," she whispered.

"He looks fine. He's being questioned about the

kidnapping of a little boy," he said, redirecting them to the present.

"What? That's impossible. He would never do such a thing."

"He also assaulted me. Tried to run me down with his car and attacked me on the beach."

"Oh, Jeremy. I am sorry. He's been so angry since he became a teenager. Ever since he turned sixteen he and Robert have been fighting. Andrew is so smart and Robert wants him to study medicine or law. But you know teenagers. Andrew has his own ideas."

Jeremy wasn't sure he could take any more.

"What ideas?" he said.

"He wants to become a Metro policeman, of all things. He was going to apply on his eighteenth birthday."

"He's not eighteen yet?"

"No, he'll turn eighteen on May twenty-second."

Which explained the need for false identification. A Metro officer, what were the chances?

"Robert argued that he should go to university and get a college education. Anyway, Andrew emptied his savings account and left two months ago. He wrote me a note, saying he'd be fine and that he was off to prove something important."

"And you haven't heard from him since?"

"A phone message every other week letting me know he's okay. I'd hoped he meant to travel

Europe, go exploring, maybe find himself. But I was afraid he might try to find you. I don't know how he did it."

"But why did he attack me?"

"I don't know. Maybe…"

"What?"

"We told him you didn't want anything to do with his life. I suppose he resents you because you didn't want him."

"Which is a lie."

"How do you know what you would have done back then? You were a brilliant boy starting college. You're so sure you would have sacrificed your future to marry me because of a mistake?"

A mistake. Just like Jeremy. God, no.

"No child is a mistake," he said.

Mercedes tapped on his window.

"I have to go, Nancy."

"I'll fly over tomorrow. What city?"

"No, I'll handle it. We'll settle this case and I'll send him home."

"Jeremy." She paused. "Take care of him. He's a good boy."

He hit the end button and opened his door.

"I'm sorry," Mercedes said.

He glanced into her wide brown eyes, brimming with compassion.

"Why are you sorry?"

"It sounds like a mess."

"I'll deal with that later."

They started up the sidewalk to the Command Center. Max greeted them at the door.

"Go back to the police station and get the boy," he ordered. "I don't care how, just get him out and bring him here. His files are encrypted. It will take Eddie hours, possibly days to get into them."

"But how will we get him out?" Mercedes asked.

"I'll take care of it," Jeremy said.

They drove back to the police station in silence, Jeremy not knowing how much of his shame he wanted to share with Mercedes. He had a son, a son who hated him because he'd been abandoned.

He couldn't blame him. Although Jeremy held Nancy responsible for this disaster, he understood her reasoning. Back then, Jeremy was interested in one thing—studying law to please his father. He was completely devoted to his goal until he'd met Nancy and had fallen in love.

He hadn't a clue it was only silly fun for her. A great inspector he'd turned out to be.

"He's really your kid, huh?" Mercedes pulled into the parking lot.

"Yes," he admitted.

"And you had no idea?"

"None."

They got out of the car and walked around to the front of the building.

"What a nasty woman," she said.

"Who, Nancy? I don't know. I would have made a horrible father."

"Says who? The older woman who let you get her pregnant? She should have known better." She squared off at him. "Don't give me that horrible father line. I've seen you with children. You're great."

"I was doing my job."

"They don't teach that at any academy I know. You're a natural." She opened the door to the station and hesitated. "It's a good thing because dealing with teenagers can be ugly. Have you got a plan?"

"He's only seventeen. I'm going to ask that he be released into his father's custody, my custody."

As they went into the quiet station, Jeremy wished he had half her confidence in his ability to be a parent. To think he'd missed it all—the boy's football games, his first attempt at riding a bike. It should have been Jeremy steadying him from behind, at least that's what he thought fathers did. Jeremy's own father had been too involved in making his next million pounds to be bothered with his son.

No child is a mistake.

Jeremy's own words haunted him. He'd been a mistake and he'd spent his entire life trying to prove himself worthy by putting away criminals and making the world a safer place.

The door to the lower level was locked. Mercedes knocked and an agent opened it. "Yes?"

"We're here to see Andrew Burke," Jeremy said.

"He's being interrogated."

"I want him released," Jeremy said. "Immediately."

"I don't care what you want." The agent started to shut the door but Jeremy shouldered it open. "He's a minor and I'm his father."

The agent pushed open the door and led them downstairs. The sounds of the interrogation filtered down the hall.

"Who took the money?" a man shouted.

"I don't know," Andrew said.

Andrew's voice had lost the earlier arrogance he'd used with Jeremy.

"Don't lie to us," the agent said. "We know you have information about the Weddle case. Start talking."

Silence.

A loud bang echoed off the walls. Jeremy pushed the agent aside and went to the cell. Andrew was pressed up against the wall, a defiant look on his face.

"What's going on?" Jeremy asked.

"Good, old-fashioned interrogation," Agent Timmons said, staring down Andrew.

"Is this boy charged with a crime?"

"Sure." Timmons glanced at Jeremy. "We'll start by charging him with your assault."

Andrew hadn't moved from his position against the wall.

"I didn't see the man's face that attacked me," Jeremy said. "I don't know that it was Andrew."

"He admitted it earlier."

"I'm not pressing charges," Jeremy added.

"What the hell?" Timmons let himself out of the cell and motioned for Jeremy to follow him into the stairwell. "Why the about-face on this kid? He was seen leaving the wine shop and he had information about the Weddles in the backpack we found. He's obviously linked to this case."

"He is. It turns out he is, in fact, my son."

Jeremy's voice hadn't changed pitch or volume when he admitted the truth, yet Mercedes noticed a flicker of emotion in his eyes.

"Your son?" Timmons said in disbelief.

"I just found out myself," Jeremy explained. "I had an affair eighteen years ago and apparently it produced that young man in there. His mother didn't think it necessary to inform me."

"Hell, that's rough. But why did he attack you on the beach?"

"He's angry. He thinks I didn't want him. He probably blames me for his whole life coming apart. That's why he's been hovering around the Weddle case. That's why he was at the wine shop today—so he could find me."

"To kill you?" Agent Timmons said.

"No, I believe he's after something else, a closure of sorts. I can't be sure until I speak with him alone."

"Feel free," Timmons said with a hand motion.

"Not here. He needs to feel safe, not threatened." He stared down the agent. "Do you have anything directly linking him to Lucas Weddle?"

"Other than the newspaper headlines we found in his backpack? No, and now you're telling me that was about you, not the boy."

"Timmons!" another FBI agent called from the top of the stairs. "The Weddles got an e-mail from someone who claims the boy is okay."

"Hell." Timmons went to the cell and unlocked the door. "Ya know kid, I don't like you," he said to Andrew. "I don't like your attitude or the way you treat your father." He glanced at Jeremy. "But I don't have enough on you. Go." Andrew got up and shuffled to the door.

Timmons grabbed him by the arm as he passed. "I'd prefer you stick close to your father so you don't mess up our investigation again, got it?"

"Yes, sir," he said.

Mercedes noticed his eyes were not apologetic, but just the opposite. They were defiant. This was going to be an interesting ride back to the office.

They filed out to the car, Jeremy leading the way. She could imagine what he must be feeling. She sensed frustration and shame. Why? This wasn't his fault.

They got in the car. "I spoke with your mother," Jeremy said.

"Did ya catch up on the last seventeen years? Or apologize for running off?"

Mercedes glanced at Jeremy. He didn't answer. Why didn't he tell the boy the truth?

"No matter," Andrew said, glancing out his window. "It's not like she'd forgive ya anyway."

Mercedes suspected he was referring to himself, the abandoned son, never forgiving his father.

"We're taking you back to the Command Center. We have your laptop and our computer expert needs your help with your encryption codes."

"You broke into my car? You're not just a delinquent father, but a thief, as well. I'd offered to help with the case. You didn't have to break the law."

They pulled up to the Command Center and headed for the front door.

Mercedes felt she needed to defend Jeremy's honor. "Actually, I broke into your car."

"No kidding?" Andrew said. "You two got something going here? Or is it my father needing a piece of ass, like he did with my mum?"

Jeremy grabbed the kid by the shoulders and slammed him against the front door. "Don't talk to her like that. You treat women with respect, you hear me?"

"What, like you did? You took off when Nancy got pregnant. Is that what you call respect?"

Jeremy shoved the boy out of the way and went inside. Andrew started after him, but Mercedes blocked him. "No way. You stay out here with me and cool down before you go in."

"You're not my mother."

"Lucky for you. If I were your mother, I'd stick a bar of soap in that snotty little mouth of yours."

"Why, for telling the truth?"

"Young man, you have no idea what the truth is."

"You don't know anything."

"No? Let's see, you find out Jeremy is your father and you decide to stalk him, not find him and ask why he wasn't around during your childhood. You're determined to become a better investigator than your father and get involved in the Weddle case but you don't find the boy, you only complicate the investigation."

"I'm good at investigating. I'll show you, on my computer."

"You're good? You're really good?" she challenged.

He nodded and shoved his hands into his jacket pockets.

"If you were that good, you would have developed a profile about Jeremy Barnes."

"I did that."

"Yeah? Did you bother to read it? If you had one ounce of brains you'd realize that Jeremy Barnes is not only an intelligent, consummate investigator, but he's also an honorable man. He has integrity and drive and puts his life in danger to save people. If you were a good investigator, you would ask yourself, 'Would a man like this abandon his child?' But you don't ask yourself this question because you're nothing but a punk with a chip on his shoulder. Time to grow up and think about someone other than yourself. Lucas Weddle is still missing. Do you want to help us?"

"Yes." He glared at her.

"Keep an open mind and maybe you'll learn something." She turned to find Jeremy standing in the doorway. He'd heard her entire rant.

"We're coming," she said, trying to keep the irritation from her voice.

She was irritated with Andrew, with this case and mostly with herself for losing it and giving him a lecture that should have come from his father.

But his father was numb. Jeremy opened the door and they went inside.

"So this is young Andrew?" Max said, walking up to the boy. "Good to meet you. I'm Max Templeton."

They shook hands. Max hesitated for a moment, then smiled, breaking the grip.

"This is Joe Spinelli, Bobby Finn and Eddie Malone." They all shook hands. "Oh, and this is Cassie."

Andrew caught his father's eye as if remembering Jeremy's comment about treating women with respect. Andrew shook hands with Cassie. "Nice to meet you."

"Likewise." She smiled at him.

Good thing they had the Blackwell team to ground the wild energy that had been flying around outside. Even the tension in Mercedes's shoulders seemed to ease a bit.

"You'll be working with Eddie," Max said. "He needs help getting into your files."

Eddie slid a chair beside him and they went to work. Mercedes noted how much the boy looked like his father from this angle.

Jeremy and Max went into his office and Mercedes followed. Max settled behind his desk. "Your son." He shook his head. "Remarkable."

"Did you know the Weddles got an e-mail stating the boy was safe?" Jeremy redirected.

"We're on top of it. You need time to process, Jeremy."

"There's nothing to process. He detests me. When we're through with him I'll put him on a plane to Heathrow."

"He doesn't detest you," Max said. "He's probably devastated because he thinks you don't love him."

Jeremy waved him off. "Never mind that. What about the e-mail?"

"I'm more worried about the second ransom request."

"The what?" Jeremy said.

"Weddles haven't told the FBI. They don't want it botched. No one knows what happened to the first bag of money. I need you two to investigate the next drop location and set up surveillance cameras so we can get a good look at him. Act like you're out for a bite to eat, nothing official."

"The Feds are going to be livid if they find out we're doing this," Mercedes warned.

"They had their chance. They muddled it," Max said. "The next drop is scheduled for tomorrow evening at the Squire Inn, a pub on the south end of town. Check it out and place surveillance cameras near the bathrooms. That's where the drop is to take place."

"Yes, sir," Mercedes said.

"I'll keep an eye on your son," he said to Jeremy.

Jeremy nodded and they walked through the Command Center. Mercedes noticed Andrew glare at his father the entire way across the room.

"I've got the surveillance equipment," Joe Spinelli offered.

They stopped at his desk and he showed them how to set up the cameras. "You have a purse?" he asked Mercedes.

"No."

"Pick one up on your way over there. The equipment is small enough to fit in a woman's medium-sized purse."

"Great, thanks," she said, taking the bundle of equipment from him.

They went outside and the sun was setting, casting an orange glow over the bustling downtown area now filled with tourists for the Wine Festival. They found a boutique and she bought a purse to hide the equipment.

"Mind if we walk, or is the purse too heavy?" Jeremy said.

"You could be a gentleman and offer to carry it for me," she joked.

He half-smiled.

"You're the only one who can make me do that," he said.

"What?"

"Make me smile under dire circumstances."

"Gee, thanks, I think."

He glanced at her with those penetrating eyes, shielded by the glasses. "I meant it as a compliment."

She smiled herself. They walked another two blocks. Sounds of a rock band echoed through the streets.

"You really let him have it back there," Jeremy said.

"I'm sorry?"

"Andrew. You scolded him like you were his mother."

"He deserved it."

"I don't know what to say to him. My own son, a complete stranger to me." He sighed. "It's ridiculous to think we could ever have a relationship."

"What, is that guilt? You have nothing to feel guilty about."

"I conceived a child and didn't live up to my responsibilities."

"You weren't even told about him. That's not your fault."

When they got to the pub it was packed with younger couples having drinks, flirting, eating dinner. It smelled of beer and popcorn.

He leaned close so she could hear him above the noise. "This is going to be madness tomorrow."

You're driving me mad right now.

Yikes! Where did that come from, chica?

"Let's start with the bathrooms." He pointed toward the back of the pub.

A waitress greeted them before they could make their way back. "Table for two?" she said.

"We're going to hit the bathroom first," Mercedes said.

"It's not a public bathroom. You have to be a paying customer."

"We're staying for dinner," Mercedes defended.

"Name?" the waitress said, expectantly.

"Barnes," Jeremy said. "Two for dinner."

The waitress allowed them to pass. They walked down the back hallway and Mercedes handed him a camera the size of a quarter. She went into the ladies' room and strategically placed hers so it blended with the sand dollar-patterned wallpaper.

They met back in the hall and she noticed a back exit and another door that read No Exit: Employees Only.

"He'll go out that way." She pointed toward the back door.

"Too obvious. What's in there, I wonder?" he nodded toward the Employees Only door.

She pulled out her pick and fiddled with the lock.

"You sure your only crime was getting caught with spray paint?" he teased.

She smiled and opened the door.

"What would you do without me?" she teased.

She locked the door and they glanced around the room. It contained wine racks, a safe and boxes of supplies.

"That's it," he said, motioning to a window in the corner. "We'll leave a camera here and place one outside, as well."

"But how will he get in if the door's locked?"

"You had no problem breaking in."

"Yeah, but I'm a pro."

He smiled again and she found herself wanting to grab him and kiss him. Instead, she pulled a small camera from the bag and placed it on a wine rack pointing toward the door.

The sound of a key turning the lock made her jump. How were they going to explain this? If they were reported to the cops, they'd find out the Weddles had been lying about another ransom demand and—

The door creaked; she panicked, wrapped her arms around Jeremy's neck and kissed him.

Chapter Twelve

She was kissing him.

And it tasted heavenly, Jeremy thought as he parted his lips and leaned into her. She was better than he'd imagined, bloody hot.

"What the hell are you doing in here?" a male voice barked from the doorway.

They broke apart, Jeremy's mind muddled with unexpected passion. Had to get ahold of his wits. He glanced at the burly man, probably a bouncer, unable to come up with a single logical answer as to why they were locked in the supply room.

"I hate you!" Mercedes cried and slapped Jeremy.

He reached up and touched his cheek in shock. Blast, she had just kissed him. She had no right to be offended that he responded the way any typical male would.

"My purse got stolen and I started to cry and he couldn't stand being seen in public with a hysterical girl, so he dragged me back here where he wouldn't be ashamed of me." She shoved her purse at the bouncer. "See? Everything is gone!" She spun on Jeremy. "It doesn't matter to you because you're a heartless ladies' man, but I've lost my wallet, my appointment book, even my lip gloss. And you don't even care."

Jeremy admired her quick thinking and her talent at convincing the man they were a romantic couple having an argument.

"How'd you get in here? The door is locked." The bouncer directed them into the hallway.

"It wasn't locked," Jeremy argued.

"It says Employees Only."

"I was hoping for some privacy, to calm her down."

"You jerk!" She lunged at him, but the bouncer caught her by the waist.

She shot Jeremy a victorious grin, but Jeremy wanted to rip the bloke's hands off her.

"Let's go," the bouncer said.

Go where? To report them to the manager?

"Barnes!" the hostess called down the hallway.

"Our table is ready," he said to the bouncer. "Take your hands off my girlfriend."

"Or what?" he threatened, plopping Mercedes down in the hallway and glaring at Jeremy.

Great, they may not be arrested for breaking and entering, but they'd surely be remembered if Jeremy and this thug got into a fight. Especially if Jeremy used his martial arts training to take him down.

Jeremy stared into his eyes. Look scared, he thought. But he couldn't bring himself to pretend this man intimidated him. Too much had happened today. He was raw from the news about Andrew… and the kiss with Mercedes.

"I'm hungry and I have no money. The least you can do is make him buy me dinner," Mercedes said to the man.

She grabbed Jeremy's hand and shot the bouncer a pitiful pout.

"Go on, get the hell out of my sight," the bouncer said, probably angry with himself for leaving the door unlocked.

Jeremy absently followed Mercedes. Surrounded by the chatter and laugher of a full pub, he couldn't even think straight.

Mercedes placed her hand to the back of his neck and for a second he thought she meant to kiss him again. Instead, she whispered in his ear. "We need to stay for dinner to make our story convincing. You know, act like we're a fight-and-make-up kind of couple."

Convincing. This was about setting up the equipment and analyzing the ransom drop.

It had nothing to do with the pain starting deep in his chest, an ache for the physical connection with this woman. He admitted to himself that it wasn't just physical. He wanted something else from her. Something he didn't dare consider.

The waitress sat them in a corner booth by the front window. The pub was loud, to be sure, but it was quieter up front.

"What can I get you to drink?" the waitress asked.

"Sparkling water, please," Jeremy said.

The waitress made a face.

"Rum and cola," Mercedes ordered.

The waitress disappeared into the mass of people. He noticed the bouncer eyeing them through the crowd.

"Give me your hand," Jeremy said.

She hesitated.

"We're being watched."

She spotted the bouncer and slid her right hand across the table. Jeremy took it and brought it to his lips. Closing his eyes, he kissed the back of her hand, then turned it over and kissed her palm. It tasted of citrus and mint and he wondered what she used on her skin that made it so soft, so seductive.

"Jeremy?" she said.

"Yes?" He opened his eyes.

She said something, but he couldn't hear it above the music.

"This is ridiculous." He got up and shifted into the booth beside her.

Panic flashed in her eyes, as if she feared what could happen between them if he got too close. He smiled, letting her know this was all part of the ruse. She relaxed and he put his arm around her shoulder.

He didn't expect her to lean into his chest.

"That was quick thinking back there, Agent Ramos," he said.

She leaned back and looked into his eyes. "I'm sorry about the slap. I wanted it to look real."

Real, like the way his heart skipped at the concerned expression in her eyes? That was very real and it scared the hell out of him.

The waitress served their drinks and they ordered dinner. Fish and chips for Jeremy and a cheeseburger for Mercedes.

"I think our spy is gone," she said, scanning the pub.

But Jeremy wanted to sit with his arm around this warm and caring woman for just a few minutes longer. Was that so wrong?

She must have read his mind, because she leaned into his chest again, tipping her face to study him. "If you talk to him, he'll understand."

"What, the bouncer?"

"Your son."

He sighed and closed his eyes. His son—a miracle or a disaster? He still wasn't sure.

He felt something touch his cheek, warm and soft. She was kissing him again. He opened his eyes and glanced to the back hallway, but the bouncer was nowhere in sight.

She was kissing him because she wanted to, not because she had to keep up the pretense.

He looked into her amazing brown eyes. "Why did you do that?"

"You looked like you needed it."

She was right. He did need her kisses and a lot more. Blast, how did he end up here, falling for a woman he couldn't possibly have?

"Talk to Andrew," she said. "Explain what happened. He can't fault you for not knowing."

"No, but he could find fault in a lot of other things."

"Like what?"

"Being married to my job, being distant," he hesitated, "being passionless."

She narrowed her eyes at him. "If that were true, you wouldn't be able to kiss like this."

She framed his cheeks with her hands and kissed him, gently at first, then she opened to him and teased at his lips with her tongue.

He lost it, turned his body to her and slid his hand to her back, pulling her close. Then it struck him that not only was he kissing a fellow agent, but he was kissing her in public, in front of a hundred strangers.

It didn't matter. For the first time in over twenty years Jeremy lost his will to micromanage every moment, every piece of his life. He wanted to kiss Mercedes until they were both dizzy with need.

The sound of someone clearing her throat shocked him back to his senses. He broke the kiss and looked up at the waitress. She slid their dinners to the table and raised an eyebrow.

"Thank you," Jeremy said.

She walked away, shaking her head.

He looked at Mercedes, whose cheeks flushed pink. "You're blushing," he said.

She glared at him. "I do not blush." She grabbed the ketchup. "Eat your dinner."

He watched her squirt ketchup, mustard and Tabasco sauce on her sandwich. She sank her teeth into the bun and closed her eyes, making a soft sound in her throat.

He was getting turned on just watching her. After a few bites, she glanced up.

"What?"

"I've never seen anyone enjoy dinner so much."

"You're making fun of me." She put her sandwich down.

"No, I'm not. I'm appreciating you."

And I'm wanting you. His thoughts had to be obvious in his eyes.

She shrugged and went back to her cheeseburger.

Then again, maybe not.

They finished their dinners, making small talk. He shared a few stories about working with the Special Crimes Initiative and she spoke mostly about her adoring little sister, bossy brothers and strict father.

"I'll never forget having to sneak out to go to a school dance with Antonio," she said.

"Your boyfriend?" he asked.

She shot him a strange smile and said, "Sure."

He knew then that she had loved this boy.

"What happened?"

"I never got caught." She leaned back in the booth. "Papi didn't even wake up when we climbed into my second story window and fell to the floor. We made quite the racket."

"We?"

She narrowed her eyes at him. "Oh, I know what you're thinking. But I was only seventeen and Antonio had no experience in the girl department. Now give him a car and he knew the name of every belt and every pipe. But he knew nothing about girls and what turned them on."

"But you taught him?"

She slugged him in the arm. "Hey, that's personal."

He wondered if Antonio was her first love.

Like Nancy had been his. At eighteen.

Andrew was going to be eighteen soon. Had he fallen in love yet? Made love to a girl?

"What's with the look?" Mercedes asked.

He stabbed a piece of fish with his fork, but had lost his appetite. "Nothing, you done?"

"Yeah."

"Let's get back to the office."

And just like that, he withdrew, as if behind a wall of bulletproof glass, and was gone again.

Was he mad because Mercedes wouldn't give him the ugly details of that night? The night that she'd almost lost her virginity to Antonio? Luckily her brother Carlos caught them before it got too out of hand.

Jeremy paid the bill and they started down the street. The sun had gone down, taking the warmth with it. A chill raced across her shoulders.

"You're cold." He put his arm around her and held her close.

It seemed so natural to be touching this man.

Kissing this man.

She sighed, knowing that this could only lead to disaster. Just like her tryst with Michael. Of course, she hadn't considered it a tryst. She'd thought at twenty-five that she'd fallen in love and found the man of her dreams. The only time she could remember blushing was when she'd made love to Michael. Although inexperienced, she'd practically attacked him in bed and he'd pointed out that usually the man leads in lovemaking. She'd backed off, thinking they had something real and honest between them.

Then she'd shown up for her shift early and caught the boys laughing and teasing Michael about slumming with a spic. Ignorant jerks.

Michael had been the biggest jerk of all. He hadn't stopped them, hadn't set them straight that he and Mercedes were in love, because, obviously, Michael wasn't in love.

Her heart broke into a million pieces that day.

Seven years later it still stung, but it was also a good lesson. Work relationships will leave you heart-broken and potentially unemployed.

She'd asked for a transfer to another district, but her sergeant rejected her request, so, she had to put up with the stares and snorts. Luckily the FBI had an opening and it probably hadn't hurt that she was Puerto Rican. For once, she welcomed the chance she'd been given because of her race and sex.

She'd thrown herself into each investigation to prove to the world that she wasn't just a pretty face.

"Tired or pensive?" Jeremy asked.

"Pensive."

"Me, too. There's so much going on with this case I can't get my bearings."

Like the way we feel about each other?

"The kidnapper gets the first ransom, but wants another?" Jeremy said.

"Unless he didn't get the first ransom."

"Let's start at the beginning. Is this an accidental drowning?"

"I doubt it. The Coast Guard hasn't found the body."

"But they found the backpack."

"True," she said.

"Is it an Internet abduction?"

"Eddie hasn't found anything to support that."

"Then a random kidnapping?"

"It doesn't feel like it."

"No, it doesn't."

They walked another block in silence. It amazed her how they thought alike, puzzling through the case and drawing the same conclusions.

"We're missing it altogether, aren't we?" she asked.

"That's what I'm thinking."

They started up the walkway to the office and he removed his arm from her shoulder. A chill rippled down her spine.

He hesitated at the door and looked into her eyes. A smile creased the corner of his mouth.

"I had fun," he said.

She guessed having fun was not something Jeremy Barnes admitted to often.

"Me, too."

He opened the door and they went inside. "Hey!" Eddie called from his desk. "Your kid here is a genius."

Andrew's expression hardened as if the reference to Jeremy being his father sickened him.

Poor kid. He hadn't a clue what was going on.

Yeah, like she did?

"Look at this." Eddie motioned to the computer.

When Jeremy leaned over to look at the screen, Andrew glared at him and started to get up. Mercedes placed her hand on his shoulder and glared right back, letting him know he was staying put. "Investigators act like professionals," she said.

He didn't move.

"The kid here found all kinds of interesting financial dirt about Weddle's close circle of friends. The Lynks' have applied for a second mortgage and the Reynolds's recently sold stock at way below the purchase price."

"Interesting," Jeremy said.

Mercedes could have imagined it, but it looked like Andrew sat a little straighter with pride.

"He also zeroed in on a few questionable e-mails. This one is a doozy."

Jeremy read the e-mail and shared it with Mercedes. It was from a grant applicant who threatened to destroy Doug Weddle and his family for ruining his life.

"This could just be a nut case," she said.

"At least it's something," Andrew said. "More than you've got."

"We would have found it sooner if we hadn't been distracted by my stalker," Jeremy said.

Andrew clenched his jaw.

The two of them were so much alike, so stubborn, Mercedes thought.

"Anyway, you've got a few suspects here." Eddie slapped his hand to a small stack of folders. "Max and Cassie are meeting with the Weddles about tomorrow's drop, Joe is following up on the wine shop snafu and Bobby went back to Mountain View to check out a lead. Max cancelled tonight's meeting. He said we could hook up in the morning around nine."

Mercedes glanced at the wall clock. It was

nearly eight. She'd spent hours with Jeremy and it felt like minutes.

"Anyway, I'm outta here," Eddie said, standing and grabbing his jacket from the chair. "Gonna get me some beer and brats."

"Me, too," Andrew said, standing.

"No ale," Jeremy ordered.

Silence sparked between them.

"Not to worry, boss," Eddie said, motioning to Andrew. "I'll take care of him. He can stay with me if he wants. I got an upgraded room by mistake." He winked.

"You sure?" Jeremy said, more to Eddie than Andrew.

It was obvious that Andrew wanted nothing to do with his father.

"No problem." Eddie turned to Andrew. "Let's bring the laptop back with us. I've got Flight Simulator VI and Renegade Soldier III on it."

"RS III isn't out for another month," Andrew said in awe.

"I know." They ambled toward the door. "See ya tomorrow," Eddie said over his shoulder.

Andrew kept walking, didn't even turn to say good-night.

Jeremy's jaw twitched at he stared at the door. "Renegade Soldier III," he muttered.

She could tell it was eating him up inside—his own son wanted nothing to do with him.

"Let's look through these e-mails," she said, grabbing half the stack and sitting at her desk. He didn't move. She glanced up. "Jeremy?"

"You're trying to distract me."

"Am I?" She leaned back in her chair.

He grabbed the other stack and sat across from her. "Thanks," he said, analyzing the first open folder.

"You're welcome." She paged through the first folder on the Lynk family. She had a hard time picturing these people having anything to do with the kidnapping. A second mortgage wasn't all that uncommon these days. Then she noticed something else.

"The Lynks' company was sold last year," she said. "Their money problems might be worse than we think."

"And they're in town, supposedly consoling their friends," Jeremy added.

She shook her head. "Nah, I can't see them as kidnappers, can you?"

She glanced up and caught him staring at her.

"People are rarely what they appear to be," he offered.

"Meaning?"

"They seem polite and loyal. But maybe it's an act."

"So they're pretending to be something they're not."

"Exactly."

She glanced back at her paperwork.

"Like you," he said.

She looked up and found him studying her again, with that same intense look. "What about me?"

"The kiss back at the pub, were you pretending? Or did something happen that neither of us had planned?"

Heat rose to her cheeks.

"You're blushing again," he said, his voice soft.

She snapped her eyes back to the paperwork. How unprofessional, blushing, not denying his suspicions that she was, in fact, falling for him.

"Mercedes?"

When he said her name with that crisp accent it drew her like a magnet. She glanced at him. His eyes had turned a warmer shade of blue.

"I'm sorry," he said. "I don't think—"

His cell phone cut him off.

"Barnes," he answered.

Good, she'd been saved from being rejected. She knew what he'd planned to say, that he didn't think it was a good idea for them to become romantically involved.

She felt like a fool.

"Where are you?" he said into his phone. He scribbled on a piece of paper. "We'll be right there."

He flipped his phone closed and stood. "Bobby's been in a car accident."

Chapter Thirteen

They picked up Bobby about twenty minutes south of town. He'd been on his way back from Mountain View when another car bumped him, sending his rental spinning off the side of the road into a ditch.

Too much of a coincidence, Mercedes thought. They were getting close to something.

"You should have called the police," Jeremy said as they headed back to town.

"What, and have them poking their noses into my investigation? No thanks."

He rubbed the side of his head where a small bruise had formed.

"Maybe we should take him to the emergency room," she said.

"No, no hospitals. I'm fine," he argued.

But his normally playful eyes looked grayed and bloodshot, his voice sounded weak as if he was fighting a cold. The adrenaline rush must have worn off.

"Tell us what you saw, exactly." Jeremy glanced into the rearview.

Mercedes turned to look at Bobby over the front seat.

"Headlights," he said. "Tall, like a truck."

She and Jeremy shared a look.

"I thought he meant to pass me, but then he slowed down, like he'd realized he was following too close. Next thing I know I'm shoved forward and the car goes flying into the ditch. Max is going to have my head," he muttered.

"Do you remember anything about the truck?" Jeremy quizzed.

"Other than he didn't stop to see if I was alive? Bloody prick." He glanced at Mercedes. "Sorry."

"I've heard worse." She smiled.

"What about the driver?" Jeremy said.

"It was pitch-black, guv. I didn't see anything."

Bobby leaned his head back against the seat. She could tell he was frustrated.

"Do we assume it's the same truck?" Jeremy said to her.

"What truck?" Bobby's eyes popped open.

"A truck nearly ran us off the road yesterday," she explained.

"And now he comes after me? How many stalkers do you have, guv?"

"What were you investigating in Mountain View?" Jeremy ignored Bobby's question.

"A lead Eddie gave me on the investment club. Paul Reynolds told me the Lynks lost thousands in a genuine stock that Doug Weddle picked as a fantasy investment. It's some sort of game, the investment club, friendly competition and all that. For some reason Lynk thought Weddle had an inside track and lost real money."

"And Reynolds?"

"He said he'd never put real money in a fantasy game. Nice chap, offered me a pint."

Jeremy eyed him.

"Okay, I accepted. I didn't want to be rude," Bobby said. "I didn't even drink half of it, guv, honest. Anyway, it seems the Lynks have a strong motive for kidnapping."

"But Lucas might recognize their voices," Mercedes said.

"They could have hired someone to snatch the kid," Bobby offered.

"Possibly," Jeremy said.

She sensed that something bothered him. They pulled into the hotel parking lot and got out of the car.

"We'll walk you in," Jeremy said.

"I'm not a bloody baby."

"No, but you're acting like a bloody wanker. Be gracious and let us help."

They walked Bobby to his room, speculating about the Lynks as suspects.

"Thanks, guv, I'm fine, truly," Bobby said, opening his door.

"Very well then." Jeremy nodded to Mercedes and they headed down the hall.

Laughter echoed off the walls as Eddie and Andrew came around the corner.

"Hey, boss," Eddie said. "What's up?"

Andrew's icy stare must have torn Jeremy apart.

"We brought Bobby home," Mercedes said. "He was in a car accident."

Eddie's smile faded. "Is he okay?"

"He's fine. A little banged up. A truck forced him off the road, possibly the same truck that tried to run us off yesterday."

"Description?" Eddie nodded to Andrew, who pulled out a small notebook.

It was almost as if he was Eddie's assistant.

"A beat-up red truck, a pickup," Mercedes said.

"Plate number?" Andrew asked.

"We didn't see it," Mercedes said.

"Bugger." Andrew shoved the notebook back into his jacket pocket.

"Well, we're off to unwind with a quick game of Renegade Soldier III. Wanna come?" Eddie offered.

Andrew glared at his father.

"No, but thank you," Jeremy said.

"See you tomorrow." Eddie led Andrew down the hall and shoved a key card into a door.

Andrew paused before going into Eddie's room.

He shot Jeremy a look of disgust. Mercedes was tempted to give him another lecture.

Eddie and Andrew disappeared into the room and the door shut with a click.

Jeremy didn't take his eyes off the door. "I've never felt more alone than in the presence of my son," he whispered.

Mercedes's heart went out to him. She understood the need to push people away, to isolate yourself.

"I'm down the hall," she said, taking him by the arm and leading him toward her room. This was not the time to deal with his angry son and the mess created by that witch Nancy. Both men needed to calm down before they attempted to work through this.

They hovered outside her room.

"You want to come in and unwind?" she asked. "I don't have Renegade Soldier but I've got a great view of the ocean."

"I'd better not."

"Oh, okay, sure." She attempted a friendly smile, but couldn't hide her disappointment. She'd fooled herself into thinking something had started between them and it had nothing to do with this investigation.

"I'll see you tomorrow then." She quickly opened her door and went inside, shutting it behind her.

"Fool."

She peeled off her work clothes. Constrictive as

hell, she thought, removing her panty hose, then her white blouse. She opened a drawer and pulled out a bright green T-shirt with pink-and-yellow flowers on the front. She turned the TV on and slipped into her tight black leggings. She pulled her hair from its ponytail and brushed it in long, steady strokes.

She should be relieved that he hadn't accepted her offer to come in and unwind. That could be dangerous; they could end up in bed. With the heady emotions pulling at him, he wouldn't know what he was doing, making love to his partner because he needed a connection, because his own son hated his guts.

But she knew why she'd be doing it. She wanted him. For no sensible reason. She wanted to pursue a relationship with this man, a man who respected her abilities as an investigator. A man she'd grown to trust.

You can't have it both ways. Either sleep with him or work with him.

Someone knocked on the door. Probably Eddie needing a third player for Renegade Soldier. She got up and looked through the peephole.

Jeremy.

She opened the door and his lost expression changed to appreciation as his gaze roamed her body. As if catching himself, he snapped his attention up to her eyes.

"Sorry. You…the outfit," he stuttered.

She enjoyed his reaction.

"What, you think I wear that suit to bed?" she joked. "Did you want something?"

Because she knew what she wanted and if he stood there another minute, she was taking it.

"I want to, ah..." Jeremy glanced away, trying not to be disrespectful when he looked at her.

"What?" she said.

She seemed irritated, Jeremy thought. She was probably exhausted.

"Nothing, sorry." Jeremy turned to leave, but she grabbed his hand.

"Get in here." She pulled him into her room and kissed him, her hands slipping under his jacket and sliding it off his shoulders.

He stroked her back, deepening the kiss. They stumbled to the bed and collapsed on the soft mattress, Mercedes on top of him. He needed this so bloody much.

No, it shouldn't be happening. This isn't a casual affair.

He wouldn't treat this woman with such disrespect.

Holding her by the shoulders, he broke the kiss. Her eyes sprung open, wide, dark and filled with need.

"What are we doing?" he asked, out of breath.

"You mean the technical term?"

"I came back to apologize for taking advantage of you earlier, for kissing you."

She climbed off of him. "Apology accepted." She planted her hands on her hips and stared at the floor.

He'd hurt her. He ran his hand through his hair. "What I meant was—"

"I understand. No explanation necessary."

"Mercedes—"

"It's fine, just go."

What had he done? Used his good sense and self-control to ruin what could have been the most amazing intimacy of his life. He knew it in his heart. He knew she'd surrender with complete abandon and maybe even teach him to do the same.

He'd only felt that way once in his life and that had ended horribly. He wanted to give it another try.

He stood and framed her face with his hands. "You are an amazing woman. I haven't wanted a woman like I want you since..."

"But, this is wrong," she finished for him. "I don't want to lose your respect."

He rubbed her cheek with his thumb. "I think you're an intelligent, savvy investigator. That will never change. But you've changed something in me. My heart is telling me that you and I, together, is promising. And for the first time in years, I'm listening to it."

He led her back to the bed and feathered kisses down to the base of her neck and across her shoulder. Her skin was soft and warm and tasted of crisp citrus.

She wrapped her arms around his neck and kissed him—a long, deep kiss that vibrated with her moan of pleasure. He wanted to pleasure her in the gentlest ways. She pulled his shirt and undershirt free of his trousers and lifted them up, over his head. Their lips only parted for a few seconds and he missed her in those seconds.

Then they were back, kissing and touching, connecting in that place reserved for lovers. She broke the kiss to pull down the covers and they fell into bed, Mercedes straddling him and ripping off her wild shirt. She ran her hands across his chest.

She leaned forward, kissing his chest, his neck, his lips. "Touch me," she whispered against his lips.

He grew hard with her demand. He cupped her breasts, brushing at her nipples with his thumbs.

She arched and whispered something in Spanish. He wasn't sure what it meant, but by the look on her face, her eyes pinched shut, her tongue dancing out to wet her lips, he knew what she wanted. And he ached for it, as well.

He ran the back of his hand across her stomach, past her waist and down. When he cupped the warmth between her legs, she cried out.

"Pants off," she demanded, rolling onto her back.

"You're the bossy one," he joked, then kneeled beside the bed and slipped off her skintight leggings. This beautiful woman writhed with anticipation of what was to come.

He took off his trousers and shorts and ran his hands along the outside of her legs, kissing the inside of her thighs and up, to that soft, magical place that made her pinch his back with wanting.

"Don't tease me anymore," she said.

"I'm not teasing you, I'm cherishing you," he said. "Every inch of you."

He licked and kissed and she grabbed him by the hair and pulled him up to lie on top of her, his heat poised to set her body on fire.

She opened her eyes and what he saw there scared the hell out of him. Just as he'd suspected—complete abandon. She was giving herself to him entirely, without reservation.

"What about a condom?" she said.

"Right." Good God, he'd almost forgotten.

Leaning over her, he reached for his trousers and grabbed his wallet. He kept a condom there, prepared for any eventuality.

"What happens if I take these off?" she asked, slipping his glasses from his face.

"I can't see."

"You don't need to see—just feel."

He could still see the need in her eyes, the hunger.

"God, you are beautiful," he whispered, slipping the condom in place.

She opened to him, thrusting her hips, making it impossible for him to do anything but fill her with his love.

They joined as one, their bodies hot with wanting, aching for release.

"Let go." She trailed her hands across his bum, pulling him closer, deeper.

He felt a connection to this woman that he'd never felt before, a connection that had less to do with their bodies and more to do with their souls. She thrust her hips, once, twice and he lost all control—all thought. He thrust forward and fell apart, a sound echoing off the walls that he didn't recognize as his own voice, a cry of surrender that ripped through his chest.

She cried out, as well, and they collapsed to the bed. Tossing the covers across her backside, he held her close, stroking her hair, thanking God for a second chance.

A chance to let go and fall into the arms of someone who could love him.

"*AY CARUMBA*," MERCEDES muttered, walking toward the Command Center. "What have you done, chica?"

Nothing, she'd done nothing wrong.

Except sleep with her boss. Or was he her partner? Her brain hurt so badly she wasn't sure what they were. But she knew they were investigators who had to focus on their case.

Jeremy had left in the middle of the night, sneaked away like a bad boy who'd had sex with his best friend's girl or something.

Or something. He was probably messed up in the head after their little tryst.

Tryst, maybe. But little was not the word to describe the sensations racing through her body with every touch, every kiss. When she woke up, her skin still tingled all over. That was a first. Even sex with Michael hadn't come close to what she and Jeremy shared.

She walked up to the Command Center, trying to keep the lightness from her step. She didn't have to broadcast the fact that she got lucky last night. No, what she shared with Jeremy was between the two of them, no one else.

When she pulled open the door, she was shocked to see Jeremy and Andrew in Max's office. Could they actually be talking?

"Hi," Cassie said.

Mercedes smiled. "Good morning."

"We'll start when Max gets here, in about ten minutes."

"How long have they been in there?" Mercedes motioned to the office where Jeremy stared out the window and Andrew fidgeted in the chair behind him.

"An hour maybe?"

She glanced at Cassie. "That long?"

"They've got a lot to talk about."

"Doesn't look like they're doing much talking."

Suddenly, Andrew shot out of his chair and stormed from the room. "He's impossible," he said, walking past them and out the front door.

Eddie walked in. "Hey, kid, what's up?"

Andrew ignored him.

"What's with him?" Eddie asked.

"He's a teenager," Jeremy said from the office door.

A few team members laughed. Mercedes studied Jeremy, waiting for him to make eye contact. He didn't.

"Ready to start?" Max said, coming into the room.

Everyone took their seats and waited.

"Where's Andrew?" he asked.

"Throwing a tantrum," Jeremy explained.

"Here's the strategy for the day," Max started.

Mercedes struggled to focus past the shame burning her insides. It was a mistake. Jeremy was embarrassed by their lovemaking. Why else would he be avoiding eye contact?

"Weddles got further instructions about the drop," Max said. "They've changed the location to one of three pancake houses. They're playing it like a treasure hunt and it's happening later this afternoon. We don't know why the change."

"So the undercover pub work last night was for nothing," Jeremy said.

Mercedes's heart sank. Lower. Lower. The kissing, the sharing of life secrets.

And he called it nothing, all part of the job.

"The kidnapper probably wants to keep everyone off balance by changing plans," Max said. "The new plan is to leave the ransom at one of three pancake houses. He'll call with the location later this morning. A team will be at each one. Spinelli and Malone will take the Pig in Blankets on the

South end of town. Jeremy and I will take the Maple House and Agents Ramos and Finn will cover the Waffle Barn."

Oh, God, they'd put her with a new partner. The writing was on the wall, in bright red spray paint—*Ramos is out because she screwed her partner.* Couldn't she ever get it right?

Being assigned a new partner was the beginning of the end. First it was reassignment, followed by busywork. She noticed that Jeremy had been paired with Max. He probably wanted Max's undivided attention when he told him how unprofessional Mercedes had been last night, making love to him, giving herself completely.

Another job lost and she'd done it to herself.

By falling for the reserved Englishman.

"We've got communications devices," Max continued. "Everyone stays in the loop on this in order to make it work. With any luck we'll have Lucas back by suppertime."

They broke off into groups, continuing their assignments. Jeremy disappeared, literally.

"So, it's you and me then, love?" Bobby said, walking up to her.

"Yep." She couldn't say anything else, couldn't utter a single word. Her heart was being ripped in two.

Silly, foolish girl.

"I'm working some leads on Internet friends, in case the Lynk angle doesn't work out," Bobby said.

"Great."

"You okay? You're lookin' a bit piqued."

"Hey, I should be asking you that question." She eyed him. "Signs of whiplash?"

"Just a headache. Nothing to worry about."

She and Bobby spent the morning and early afternoon on Internet leads. There was no sign of Jeremy since earlier in the day and no sign of his son, either. Maybe he wasn't avoiding her. Maybe he was spending quality time with Andrew.

Yeah, and if you believe that, you really are a fool.

At four o'clock, Agent Spinelli set them up with listening devices—an earpiece and small microphone to attach to their jackets.

"Agent Ramos?"

She glanced up into Jeremy's eyes, shocked that he'd actually spoken to her.

"Yes, Agent Barnes?"

He opened his mouth and closed it. "Be careful."

"You, too."

She sensed he wanted to say more.

Wishful thinking, chica. Stupid, wishful thinking.

JEREMY WATCHED MERCEDES and Bobby leave the office, Mercedes wearing an odd expression on her face. He couldn't read her today, which was a first.

He couldn't think of one intelligent thing to say

to her after their amazing night. Yet she seemed unaffected by their lovemaking. Or was she ashamed?

No, she shouldn't be. Jeremy had been the one to cross that line.

Maybe she was angry because he'd left in the middle of the night. But he'd awakened with a start, something poking at his subconscious, driving him out of bed and to the office to sift through files.

Unfortunately he hadn't found anything solid. He would have been better off lounging in her arms.

Now what are you thinking about? Haven't you got enough complications without adding a romantic relationship to the mix?

"You're going to hurt yourself, mate," Max said, walking up to him. "You're thinking too hard. Let's go have some cakes."

"Right."

Max gave Cassie a kiss and she settled behind a desk.

Jeremy wished he could have given Mercedes a kiss like that, a quick one for luck. But he wasn't sure what to make of their relationship; he didn't want to assume anything.

He wished deep in his heart that she felt the same way he did—that maybe, possibly, she'd developed feelings for him.

He'd asked Max for the reassignment because he wanted to pair a strong agent like Mercedes with

Bobby, a man who might still be rattled by the car accident last night.

Jeremy could also use a little distance from his beautiful partner to get his perspective, to make sense of it all, so he'd know what to say when the time was right.

Like he knew what to say to Andrew?

He and the boy had gone at it this morning, Jeremy telling his son he belonged back home with his mother and Andrew arguing with him. The teenager still didn't know the whole truth, and Jeremy didn't see any sense in telling him. Jeremy wanted to do the right thing by Andrew, not confuse him any further.

The boy was meant to grow up with his family, attend university and live his life in England.

He and Max went to the Maple House and stood in line. Jeremy actually had an appetite this morning.

"A lot has happened the past few days," Max said. "You all right?"

"Fine."

"That's rubbish and you know it."

Jeremy smiled. "I guess you know me pretty well."

"Finding out you have a son after all these years would throw anyone off course."

"He hates me."

"So did I." He smiled. "But I warmed to you. He will, too. What about Agent Ramos?"

"What about her?"

"You still want her fired?"

"No, she's an excellent agent."

"I'm glad you think so." Max smiled.

"Bugger off," Jeremy said.

"What?" Max placed an open palm to his chest. "If you ask me, I think you make a brilliant team. You and Agent Ramos."

"I don't remember asking you," Jeremy shot back.

Max smiled.

"Stop grinning like a fool," Jeremy teased. He glanced out the restaurant window and noticed the bully, Brad Reynolds, race across the parking lot.

"Odd," Jeremy said.

"What?" Max strained to see what Jeremy was looking at.

"I'll be right back." Jeremy went outside and followed the boy, calling his name.

Something about the Reynolds family had been bothering him, but he wasn't sure what.

"Brad Reynolds!" he called. The boy disappeared down a flight of stairs leading to the beach. Jeremy followed, but by the time he reached the sand the boy had vanished.

Walking thirty or so meters, he glanced up at the houses, perched on the bluff. That's when he spotted it—a red pickup in a grassy lot. He climbed up the wooden steps to get a better look.

Then it struck him. That nagging sensation that woke him in the early hours—Paul Reynolds, good friend, who couldn't afford a family vacation in Hawaii, but was buying property on the coast?

Reynolds had given Bobby a pint last night. Could he have laced it with something that dulled Bobby's reactions, making it easier to lose control of his vehicle?

"I've got something," Jeremy said into the communications device.

No response. Blast, he must be out of range. He reached the top of the bluff and approached the truck. He peered inside, hoping to find something identifying the owner.

He heard the crunch of shoes on gravel, then a sharp pain cracked against his skull. He fell to the ground, started to get up and wavered. Something pounded against his back. He slammed against the hard earth and passed out.

Chapter Fourteen

The chill woke him. His body shivered to regulate his temperature. Rhythmic dripping echoed in his ears. He opened his eyes but only saw black.

Then he heard the sound of a sniffling child.

A soft glow suddenly lit the area and a child stared back at him—Lucas Weddle.

Good God, he was dead and had joined Lucas in heaven. Wait a second, it was awfully cold and wet up here.

"Hey, you're finally awake," the boy said.

"Lucas?"

"I tried to save you." He glanced at his shoes. "Sorry, I kinda messed it up."

Jeremy blinked and sat up, hugging his midsection to warm himself. "Save me?"

"Sure. I saw you get dumped in this hole so I came down to save you, only the line came loose so we're stuck down here."

"Why didn't you call the police?"

"Because they'll arrest me for running away."

"You weren't kidnapped?"

"Nnnnooo," he said. "I'm on a mission to prove I can take care of myself in the wilderness. And I did pretty good, too, until I tried saving you."

The boy was alive and unhurt. Relief washed over Jeremy.

"Why didn't you inform your parents about your mission?"

"Dad would only tell me I'm too young, or too inexperienced, or not smart enough or whatever. We went camping last month and he couldn't even build a fire."

"Your parents have been desperately worried about you."

"They shouldn't be. I left them a note. Unless…"

"What?"

"Unless Natalia stole it. She's always getting into my stuff. But it doesn't matter. I sent them an e-mail a few days ago, from a new account I set up on my BlackBerry."

An e-mail from an unknown sender. It probably went right into the spam folder.

"Lucas, where have you been this past week?"

"Camping."

"Alone?"

"Uh-huh. But yesterday I spotted my picture on a lamppost and I knew I was in trouble. I don't want to go to jail."

"They won't send you to jail for staying away from home. But your parents are worried sick."

"Mom, maybe. Dad doesn't care."

Jeremy hugged his chest tighter. His fingers were growing numb with the chill. "I'm sure your father cares. He loves you."

"Love is for girls." Lucas waved him off.

Jeremy realized Lucas was trying to prove something to his father, earn his respect, maybe even earn his love.

Jeremy knew that feeling, wanting it so badly you'd do practically anything.

Like pursue a career in law.

Or run away from home.

All for a father's love.

Suddenly Jeremy hoped for another chance with Andrew.

And Mercedes.

She'd loved him last night, and not just with her body. He could feel something growing between them, a connection he'd never felt with another woman—a connection that eased the ache in his chest.

"We need to get out of here." Jeremy stood up. His legs were stiff. "How long have I been out?"

"I don't know. A while. It's dark outside."

He assumed the money drop had been made, Reynolds got away free and clear and Jeremy sat in this mud hole, unable to expose him.

He tried to climb up the side of the hole, got about three feet, then lost his footing and fell to the muddy earth.

"Don't worry. Metro 22 will find us," Lucas said. "He's with British Intelligence. We've been e-mailing since yesterday."

Great, they were stuck in this hole and the only one who knew their location was a phantom e-mailer who probably lived in Tokyo.

"Lucas," Jeremy started, then decided not to scare the boy. He studied their prison. It had to be ten feet deep.

"I know what you're thinking," the boy said.

Jeremy glanced at him.

"You think I don't know what I'm talking about because I'm just a kid."

"No, I was considering a backup plan in case Metro 22 gets delayed," Jeremy said. "When did you e-mail him?"

"A few hours ago. But I didn't have our exact location so it might take him a while to find us."

Like forever.

"I'm hungry." Lucas opened a backpack. "Want a protein bar?"

"Where did you get that?" Jeremy said. "The Coast Guard found your school pack floating in the ocean."

"That's for kids. Did you see that red dinosaur on it? I bought this when I was on the field trip."

Lucas handed him a protein bar and Jeremy took a bite.

He'd need his strength to get out of this one.

A few minutes passed. "How about we surprise Metro 22 and figure a way out of here? How did you end up down here again?"

"I climbed down, checked your pulse, then my line mysteriously came undone. Here." He picked it up and handed it to Jeremy.

"Up for a little climbing?"

"Sure." The boy's eyes lit up.

Jeremy tied the line around Lucas's waist, knelt down and said, "Come on, up on my shoulders."

With careful balance, Jeremy steadied Lucas, then stood, slowly.

"Hey, I'm almost to the top!" Lucas cried.

"Keep steady."

"A little more, just a little more."

"I'm going to give you a push," Jeremy said. "Ready?"

"Ready."

"On three." Jeremy gripped the boy's trainers and counted. "One, two, three!"

Jeremy pushed and Lucas climbed out. "You did it! Awesome!" Lucas said, looking down at Jeremy. "Stay there."

Right, and where would he go? A second later the boy's line dropped into the hole.

"I attached it to a tree," Lucas said.

Jeremy pulled himself up and out. They followed a trail through the woods, Jeremy leaning on the boy for support. His head ached from being knocked out earlier.

"How did you happen to see the man drop me into the hole?" he asked.

"Actually, I've been watching him. He's a friend of my dad's and I don't trust him."

"Paul Reynolds?"

"That's him. And his son is a complete, uh…" He glanced at Jeremy.

"He's a wanker." Jeremy smiled.

"Nice word," Lucas said in awe.

"How far do you think we are from town?"

"Not that far. Why, are you hungry?" He hesitated to open his backpack.

"Let's get you safe first. I can wait."

"Okay."

"Hey, look!" Lucas pointed.

A flashlight winked at them through the woods.

He put his arm around the boy. "Keep quiet. It might be Reynolds."

"Einstein 10, you out there?" a voice called.

"It's Metro 22." Lucas grinned at Jeremy.

"I'm here, Metro 22!" Lucas called back.

"Keep talkin', mate, so I can find ya."

That voice, that accent, it sounded like…

"Over here, we're over here!" Lucas called out.

The boy rushed down the path and into the arms of Metro 22—Andrew.

"It's okay. I found ya." He glanced up at Jeremy. "You look like hell."

"Thanks."

"I've got 'em," Andrew said into a radio. "About twenty meters off the Timbercreek parking lot, trail *A*. I'm bringing them back to the lot."

He looked older, like a man, not the angry boy who'd been cornered in the jail cell.

"You need a hand?" Andrew offered.

It was the first pleasant thing he'd said to Jeremy. "I can manage."

They hiked through the woods, Andrew walking alongside Lucas Weddle.

"Why'd you run away, Einstein?" Andrew asked Lucas.

"I wanted to show everyone I'm a man."

"And you are, for sure. Thanks for saving that bloke back there." He jerked his thumb toward Jeremy. "He's my dad."

Jeremy's heart skipped.

They approached the clearing and the team rushed to greet them, asking questions and filling Jeremy in on what had happened.

The team figured out what Jeremy had—that Paul Reynolds was their key suspect. They found him and turned him over to the police. He never had Lucas, but had banked on the boy being dead and the body not being found until he'd made off with the ransom. Both of them. He'd taken the wine shop ransom and had set up the pancake house ransom as a decoy, to keep Blackwell's agents busy so he could set up a ransom drop with the Weddles directly.

When the team found Paul Reynolds he was heading to the airport planning to travel using a stolen identity. In financial ruin, he was leaving it all behind, even his wife and son.

Everyone threw in a comment here and there—Eddie, Max, Spinelli, Bobby and even Cassie.

But not Mercedes, she kept quiet, relief spreading across her face. And sadness?

Someone put a wool blanket around Jeremy's shoulders. Andrew.

"Thank you," Jeremy said, looking into his son's blue eyes. His expression had changed since the first time they'd met. What was once hatred had softened to concern.

Max knelt beside Lucas. "Little Lucas, aren't you the smart one? You saved my agent for me."

"I'm not all that little," he said.

"No, you're really not."

A car raced into the parking lot, followed by two patrol cars. The Weddles jumped out of their sedan and ran to Lucas.

"Oh, my God," Mrs. Weddle said over and over again.

"Lucas David Weddle, I can't believe you put us through this," his father scolded.

The boy hugged his mom, tears streaming down his face. "Don't cry, Mom. I'm okay."

Jeremy touched Mr. Weddle's shoulder. "He did it for you. He was trying to prove he was worthy of your attention."

Doug Weddle's gaze drifted from Jeremy to his son.

"Hell," he whispered, then hugged both his wife and child.

Jeremy smiled to himself. A family. They were okay. An ache filled his chest.

The Weddles went to their car and a police officer approached. "We'll need a statement," he said to Jeremy.

"Ah, let the poor man rest." Andrew got between them. "He's been through hell."

The cop nodded at Jeremy. "Tomorrow morning?"

"Sure."

"Let's get back, then." Max motioned for Bobby to drive.

They piled into the minivan and headed to the hotel, Max explaining how they came to the same conclusion that Jeremy had and found Paul Reynolds trying to make off with the ransom. Apparently Paul Reynolds felt he deserved Weddle's money because he'd followed the man's investment advice.

"Hospital or hotel?" Max said to Jeremy.

"My hotel room. I could use about twenty hours of sleep."

They pulled into the parking lot. Andrew reached for Jeremy's arm to steady him.

"I'm not completely incapable," Jeremy joked, but truthfully he enjoyed the attention.

Mercedes got out and kept her distance, walking ahead of the group. She disappeared into the hotel.

Something was off. He'd talk to her tomorrow after a good night's sleep.

"Good night, mate," Max said, an arm around Cassie.

"It's too early," Bobby said. "Who's up for a pint?"

"Count me in," Spinelli said.

Eddie glanced at Andrew, as if he didn't want to leave him behind.

"Go on," Andrew said. "I'll look after the old man."

The three men left and Andrew helped Jeremy to his room.

"Nancy says hi," Andrew said.

Jeremy stopped and searched into his son's eyes. "I never would have left you."

The boy shot him a half-smile. "Let's talk about it tomorrow, after you're feeling better."

Andrew opened the hotel room door and led Jeremy to a chair with a view of the ocean. "I'll get you some dry clothes."

"Andrew?"

"Sir?"

"Good job, tonight."

"Thanks."

"So, you want to join the Met?"

"Unless I get a better offer."

Chapter Fifteen

"Running never solved anything. I should know," Max said.

Mercedes shifted from one foot to the other. "I'm not running, sir. Blackwell isn't a good fit for me."

"Is this about Jeremy?"

Jeremy. Right, the man she'd mistakenly given her heart to and lost her self-respect in the process.

"Was he that hard to work with?" Templeton quizzed.

"He was fine."

And he was. Fine, loving, compassionate.

"I think I'm better suited to the federal agencies."

Her heart broke with the lie. She'd wanted to work for a private firm, for a group like Blackwell that acted like a family as much as an investigative team.

"Thank you for the opportunity," she said.

They shook hands.

"I'm sorry you're leaving. I thought you had real promise."

"Thanks."

She went to her desk and slipped a few personal things into her briefcase. Getting here before the rest of them had been her plan. She knew Templeton had told everyone to sleep in before the wrap up briefing. She hoped to be gone before the rest of the team got here.

Before Jeremy showed up.

She didn't know if she could stand it, looking into those blue eyes, now devoid of any professional respect. It was to be expected. They could never look at each other the same way after having such amazing sex.

But it wasn't just amazing sex. Not for her.

"You're leaving?" Jeremy said.

She jumped at the sound of his voice and turned to greet him. He looked rested but worn down. She wanted to hold him. She shut her briefcase. "You should be taking it easy."

"I asked you a question."

"I'm going to enjoy the rest of my leave from the FBI and go to Europe or something."

In truth, she was lost. She wasn't sure how she'd ended up here again, ruining her chances with Blackwell.

That's a lie. She knew exactly how she'd ended up here. She'd fallen for her partner.

"It's been great working with you." She shook

his hand, grabbed her briefcase and headed out the front door.

For a minute she thought she'd make it out in one piece, that he wouldn't follow her and add to her growing embarrassment.

He caught up to her on the sidewalk. "I want you to tell me what this is really about."

"Look, you've got a lot on your plate right now and I don't want to add to it."

"So you're leaving out of concern for me?" His amazing eyes narrowed in disbelief.

"Basically," she said.

"You promised honesty. I want it now."

"I need to go."

"You need to talk to me. Is it Andrew? Is that what's scaring you away?"

"No, Jeremy, not at all. He's a good kid."

"Then what?"

"Let's not do this."

"Why not? I may never see you again."

"Jeremy, I'm sorry, okay? The other night was a mistake."

"I scared you off, didn't I?"

She touched his cheek. "No, it's just, well, you can't help but feel differently about me and I understand."

"You're not making sense."

"You said you wouldn't lose respect for me but I see it in your eyes. You don't look at me the same way.

You barely look at me at all. When you reassigned me to partner with Bobby, I got the message." She paused. "And to be honest, I can't keep working around you, seeing that look in your eyes. I've got to go."

She kissed him on the cheek. Work or love. She could never have both.

"Mercedes?" he said.

She took a step back.

"Yes?"

"I requested that you be assigned to Bobby because I wasn't sure he had completely recovered from the car accident. I paired him with a strong, sharp agent for everyone's benefit. To help the team."

Could it be?

"And that look in my eyes, you may think it's disappointment, but in reality, it's fear. I'm terrified because I'm feeling things for you—and I've known you only a short time—which is so unlike me. I've only felt this once before and it was a bloody mess and now I've got a teenager to contend with who won't listen to a thing I say and…I'm rambling."

She smiled. "It's okay, I like the sound of your voice."

"Do you like it enough to stay?"

"Jeremy." Her gaze drifted to the sidewalk.

With his forefinger and thumb, he tipped her chin and looked into her eyes. "You can have it all—work and romance. Look at Max and Cassie. Besides, you make me smile. No one else can do that."

And she knew at that moment that she couldn't leave, couldn't walk away from this man just because they worked together.

"So, you're keeping me around for the entertainment factor?" she teased.

"I want you around because you're an amazing investigator." He hesitated. "And you watch out for me."

"Ah, I know the truth. You want me around because of my good luck."

She looped her arm through his and led him back to the Command Center.

"Want to give the lottery another go?" he asked. "Maybe you could beat your twelve-dollar jackpot."

"Nah, I've already won enough today."

* * * * *

Happily ever after is just the beginning....

Turn the page for a sneak preview of
A HEARTBEAT AWAY
by
Eleanor Jones

Special? A prickle ran down my neck and my heart started to beat in my ears. Was today really special?

"Tuck in," he ordered.

I turned my attention to the feast that he had spread out on the ground. Thick, home-cooked-ham sandwiches, sausage rolls fresh from the oven and a huge variety of mouthwatering scones and pastries. Hunger pangs took over and I closed my eyes and bit into soft homemade bread.

When we were finally finished, I lay back against the bluebells with a groan, clutching my stomach.

Daniel laughed. "Your eyes are bigger than your stomach," he told me.

I leaned across to deliver a punch to his arm, but he rolled away and when my fist met fresh air I collapsed in a fit of giggles before relaxing on my back and staring up into the flawless blue sky. We lay like that for quite a while, Daniel and I, side by side in companionable silence, until he stretched out his hand in an arc that encompassed the whole area.

"Don't you think that this is the most beautiful place in the entire world?"

His voice held a passion that echoed my own feelings and I rose onto my elbow and picked a buttercup to hide the emotion that clogged my throat.

"Roll over onto your back," I urged, prodding him with my forefinger. He obliged with a broad grin, and I reached across to place the yellow flower beneath his chin.

"Now, let us see if you like butter."

When a yellow light shone on the tanned skin below his jaw, I laughed.

"There…you do."

For an instant our eyes met, and I had the strangest sense that I was drowning in those honey-brown depths. The scent of bluebells engulfed me. A roaring filled my ears and then, unexpectedly, in one smooth movement Daniel rolled me onto my back and plucked a buttercup of his own.

"And do *you* like butter, Lucy McTavish?" he

asked. When he placed the flower against my skin, time stood still.

His long lean body was suspended over mine, pinning me against the grass. Daniel…dear, comfortable, familiar Daniel was suddenly bringing out in me the strangest sensations.

"Do you, Lucy McTavish?" he asked again, his voice low and vibrant.

My eyes flickered toward his, the whisper of a sigh escaped my lips and although a strange lethargy had crept into my limbs, I somehow felt as if all my nerve endings were on fire. He felt it, too—I could see it in his warm brown eyes. And when he lowered his face to mine, it seemed to me the most natural thing in the world.

None of the kisses I had ever experienced could have even begun to prepare me for the feel of Daniel's lips on mine. My entire body floated on a tide of ecstasy that shut out everything but his soft, warm mouth and I knew that this was what I had been waiting for the whole of my life.

"Oh, Lucy." He pulled away to look into my eyes. "Why haven't we done this before?"

Holding his gaze, I gently touched his cheek, then I curled my fingers through the short thick hair at the base of his skull, overwhelmed by the longing to drown again in the sensations that flooded our bodies. And when his long tanned fingers crept across my tingling skin, I knew I could deny him nothing.

* * * * *

Be sure to look for
A HEARTBEAT AWAY,
available February 27, 2007.

And look, too, for
THE DEPTH OF LOVE
by Margot Early,
the story of a couple who must learn that love comes in many guises—and in the end it's the only thing that counts.

Hearts racing
Blood pumping
Pulses accelerating

Falling in love can be a blur...especially at *180 mph!*

So if you crave the thrill of the chase—on and off the track—you'll love

SPEED DATING

by Nancy Warren!

Receive $1.00 off

SPEED DATING
or any other Harlequin NASCAR book.

Coupon expires December 31, 2007. Redeemable at participating retail outlets in the U.S. only. Limit one coupon per customer.

RETAILER: Harlequin Enterprises Ltd. will pay the face value of this coupon plus 8 cents if submitted by the customer for this specified product only. Any other use constitutes fraud. Coupon is nonassignable. Void if taxed, prohibited or restricted by law. Void if copied. Consumer must pay for any government taxes. Mail to Harlequin Enterprises Ltd., P.O. Box 880478, El Paso, TX 88588-0478, U.S.A. Cash value 1/100 cents. Limit one coupon per customer. Valid in the U.S. only.

113854

5 65373 00076 2 (8100) 0 11385

NASCPNUS

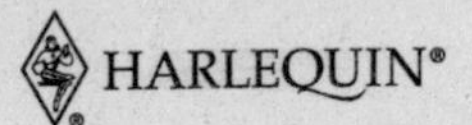

INTRIGUE®

COMING NEXT MONTH

#975 24/7 by Joanna Wayne
Bodyguards Unlimited, Denver, CO (Book 1 of 6)
The newest Harlequin Intrigue continuity, *Bodyguards Unlimited,* kicks off with a story of a first love rekindled. Jack Sanders provides around-the-clock protection, and Kelly Warner and her daughter will need every minute of it if they hope to survive the week.

#976 A NECESSARY RISK by Kathleen Long
Jessica Parker's only chance lies with Detective Zachary Thomas. But is his grim determination enough to spur her into exposing the greed spreading through the medical community—at the cost of patients' lives?

#977 JUSTICE FOR A RANGER by Rita Herron
The Silver Star of Texas (Book 3 of 3)
Texas Ranger Cole McKinney came to Justice to help his half brothers, but kindred spirit Joey Hendricks is enough to keep him there—if the secrets they uncover don't tear apart their two families first.

#978 PROTECTIVE CONFINEMENT by Cassie Miles
Safe House: Mesa Verde (Book 1 of 2)
Special Agent Dash Adams has one simple assignment: protect Cara Messinger. But the Navajo safe house's close quarters are an easy place to complicate affairs of the heart.

#979 WHO'S BEEN SLEEPING IN MY BED?
by Shawna Delacorte
Reece Covington returns to his cabin to find a woman he's never met asleep there. But as he unravels the mysterious Brandi Doyle, will he like the answers she supplies?

#980 MISS FAIRMONT AND THE GENTLEMAN INVESTIGATOR by Pat White
The Blackwell Group (Book 3 of 3)
When Grace Fairmont's trip abroad goes awry, she's lucky to have bad boy Bobby Finn looking after her. But can he protect the American girl from the one thing he's best at causing—trouble?